EVOLUTION'S CHILD - THREAD
Republic of Luna

December 2092

Charles Lee Lesher

We must question the story logic of having an all-knowing all-powerful God, who creates faulty Humans, and then blames them for his own mistakes."

Gene Roddenberry (1921-1991)

Republic of Luna

SHADOW WAR TRILOGY

File Compilation: 2015
ISBN: 978-1-938586-08-8
Kindle ISBN 978-1-938586-03-3

Shadow War Trilogy
Republic of Luna

Book 3: Evolution's Child - Thread

Science of the Republic

Some Things About Chuck

Preamble

In a century filled with strife, the dogs of war are gathering once more. By late 2092, climate change and war have devastated the planet. Even thinned by bloodshed, famine, and disease, Earth's population exceeds 10 billion. Food and water are in short supply, refugee's number in the hundreds of millions and lawlessness abounds. Humanity is in turmoil.

Religious zealots exploit this despair, claiming it's God's punishment for man's misdeeds. Within the North American Federation, Christian theocracy displaced democracy, plunging once proud America into a Dark Age. On the other side of the planet, the Islamic Brotherhood controls a third of the world from Indonesia, across Asia and the Middle East and well onto the African continent, India the only holdout. China, the leading space faring nation on Earth, allies with the Brotherhood providing them with science and technology for a price. Only within the European Union is there still a semblance of individual freedom. The nations of the world align along sectarian lines as global violence escalates.

In sharp contrast, the Republic of Luna is a technocratic society where information flows freely and nothing is secret, a place governed by humanism and the laws of science. Out of necessity, life on an airless world burrows deep underground and to stay alive, Lunarians unlock nature's deepest secrets, gaining mastery over the genetic foundations of life itself. In doing so, they become the first true extraterrestrials.

From Washington to Rome to Mecca, when Earth's theists learn of the Lunarians meddling in human genetics, they denounce them as abominations. Prince Ahmed Mohammed Al Zarqowi, Caliph of the Islamic Brotherhood, believes he can hide behind this turmoil to attack Luna with impunity and create humanity's first multi-planet empire. To the Caliph this is simply the next step in a plan to bring an unbelieving world under Islamic Law. He unleashes forces intent on destroying the Republic before it's a half-century-old.

The Players

Quan Kiai

» Captain Kitajima Osaka
» Master Sergeant Susan Hackling
» Doctor Howard Grady
» Lieutenant Tempel Dugan
» Lieutenant Tatiana Tushar
» Sergeant Consuela Navarro
» Sergeant John Kipper
» S.I.T. Angel Lopez
» S.I.T. Samantha Odegaard
» Officer Lei Cheung
» Officer Brice Guyart
» Officer Marcel Piqualow
» Officer Karl Svensson
» Officer Corazon Montano
» Officer Karyl Stormberg
» Officer Zoey Tanaka
» Officer Alonzo Tushar

Major Players

❋ Analyst Lazarus Sheffield
❋ Captain Lindsey Marquest
❋ Pilot Nell Goddard
❋ Councilor Abigail O'Neil Dugan
❋ Security Chief Corso Dugan
❋ Officer Cristobal Calatrava
❋ Magi

Islamic Brotherhood

☾ Mohammed Basayev
☾ Imam Nassah Bakr
☾ Commander Ghafour
☾ Major General Abdel Salam Arif
☾ Minister Hasin bin Aunker
☾ Captain Mustafa Malik
☾ Havildar Anwar Jafa
☾ Dalal

Minor Players

☼ Isaac Crenshaw
☼ Constance Haig
☼ Tara Dugan
☼ Mallory Higgins
☼ Lee Chin
☼ Justine Harman
☼ Nicole Dugan
☼ Elizabeth Dugan
☼ Krystin Dugan
☼ Skylor Dugan
☼ Jordan Dugan
☼ Jamie Dugan
☼ Ben Dugan
☼ Zachary Taylor
☼ Yang Lee
☼ Chen Zhi
☼ Odessa Simpson
☼ Zechariah Hargrove

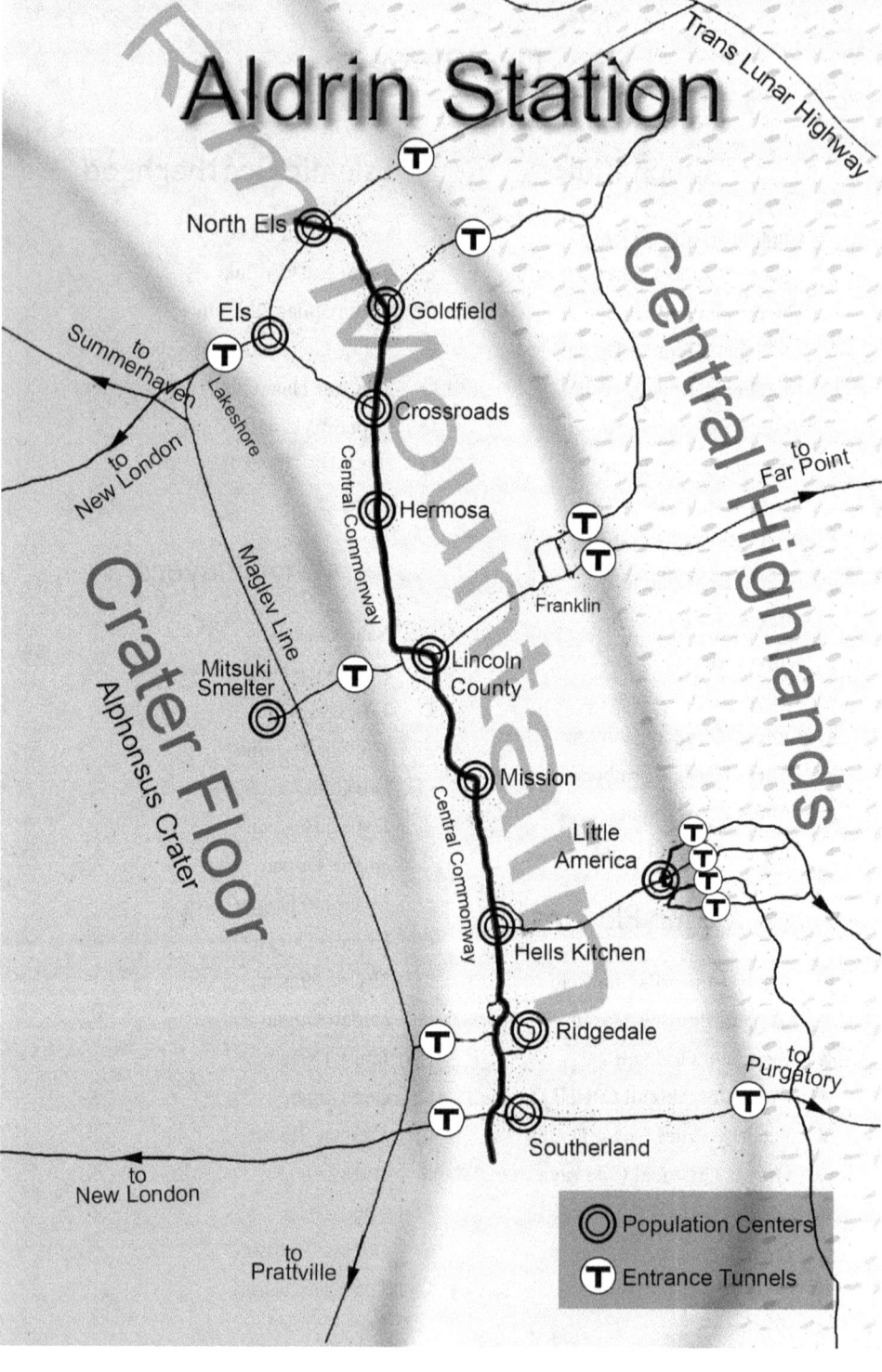

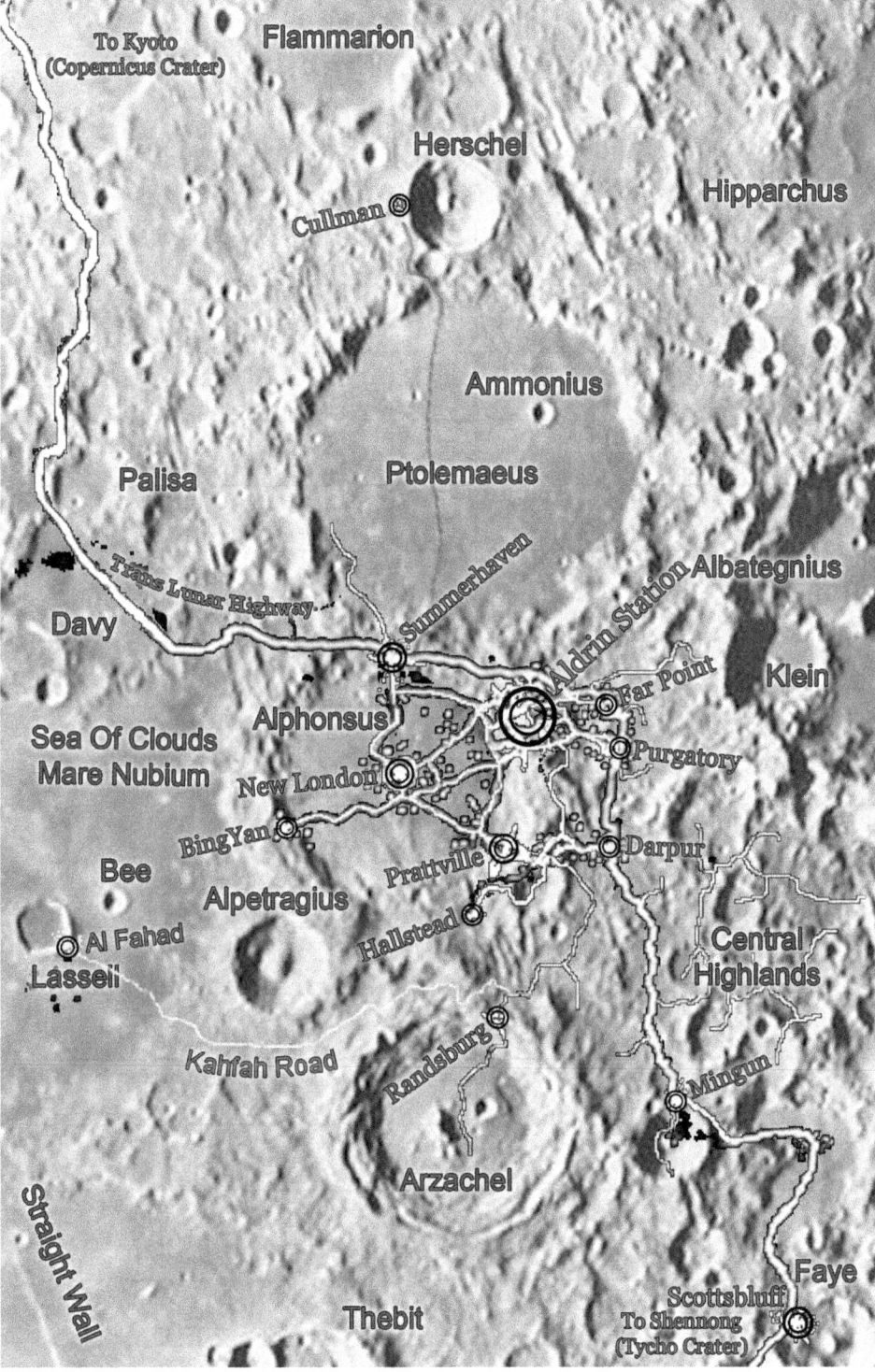

21ˢᵗ Century Timeline

HISTORICAL DETAIL	YEAR	HISTORICAL DETAIL
Abigail Katee O'Neil 10/15/99	1999	World population tops 6 billion
USS Cole attack kills 17	2000	India's population tops 1 billion
Pres: George Bush	2001	9/11/01 WTC destroyed kills 2996
Planetoid Quaoar is discovered	2002	US invades Afghanistan
1st full human genetic sequence	2003	US invades Iraq
France closes their last coal mine	2004	Asian Tsunami kills >225,000
Genetic therapy improves	2005	Hurricane Katrina kills >1300
Tree of Life project begins	2006	North Korea tests long-range missile
Human Epigenome Project	2007	Global climate change hotly debated
World economy plunges; Cloned organs	2008	Pres. Barack Obama (1st black president)
Iceland declares bankruptcy	2009	Iran launches first satalite
DNA Base Sequencer (DBS)	2010	Drought devastates southern US
Western Space Command	2011	ISS is militarized; Coalition of Christian Citizens
Orbital Nonproliferation Treaty	2012	World population tops 7 billion
Pope Francis	2013	Boston Bomding (3)
Type 3 superconductors discovered	2014	Trial of the Century
First magnetoplasma thruster	2015	EU invades South Africa
China est. Shennong	2016	Pres. Hillary Clinton (1st woman president)
9/11 Houston nuked kills >4 million	2017	Clinton signs North American Free Trade Pact
Powersat beams energy to Earth	2018	Rising sea levels top 30 cm
Longbow Mass Driver operational	2019	North American Federation formed (NAF)
NAF/EU/Japan Lagrange One (L1)	2020	American Church of the Trinity (ACT)
Japan est. Kyoto, Luna	2021	ACT rally 1.5M anti-genetics
S Korea est. Hyundai (L4)	2022	NAF outlaws all genetic research
Meteor kills 19 in Kyoto	2023	George Farcain becomes a Deacon in ACT
NAF/EU/China est. Aldrin Station	2024	Pres. Jesus Martinez (1st Latino president)
India est. Kundara	2025	EU occupies New London, Luna
NAF and EU establish Taurus (L5)	2026	NAF builds orbital battlestation
China est. Far Point Mine	2027	Rising sea levels top 75 cm
EU est. Johanson	2028	China, EU build battlestations
Japan est. Ishikawajima	2029	Great Exodus begins, Luna population grows
Shennong absorbs Ishikawajima	2030	NAF outlaws all biotronic research
Japan builds battlestation	2031	EU restricts biotronic research
India est. Darpur Mine	2032	Pres George Farcain AKA, The Pope
EU est. Purgatory Deep Hole	2033	United Nations bans human genetics

Historical Detail	Year	Historical Detail
Shennong absorbs Kundara	2034	British hospital bombed (117)
China est. Mingun Mine	2035	NAF outlaws football, boxing
Calconn presented to the world	2036	Chinese Unification; NAF absorbs Mexico
Mingun Mine, Central Highlands	2037	President Farcain assassinated; VP John Paul takes office
Expeditions to Mars and Asteroids	2038	John Paul is elected President at age 42
Paradise asteroid discovered	2039	NAF hospital bombed (53); NAF absorbs Cuba
Rising sea levels top 2 meters	2040	Japan admits to UN violations
Israel builds battlestation	2041	Japanese genetic clinic bombed (21)
After 40 yrs NAF leaves Middle East	2042	Islamic Brotherhood (IB) forms, JP reelected (46)
Lindsey Marquest 10/12/43	2043	President John Paul forms Reformation Party
Shennong absorbs Johanson	2044	ACT joins Reformation Party
China begins selling arms to the IB	2045	Japanese Hospital bombed (191)
Egypt sells weapons to South Africa	2046	IB attacks Israel and is rebuffed; JP reelected (50)
World condemns IB	2047	China brokers the Saudi Accord
R.W. McCoy first multi-trillionare	2048	Rising sea levels top 4.5 meters; US revises the Bill of Rights
India lays keel for the ISS Shakti	2049	Venice is abandoned; Presidential term limits abolished
1st Lunarian visor mass produced	2050	IB builds Mogadishu spaceport; JP reelected (54)
Miami is abandoned	2051	IB buys battlestation from Hyundai
Lunarians produce first Zettasphere	2052	Protests grow over Constitutional Issue
Fair Access becomes world law	2053	Boston Massacre (56 dead)
First permanent Mars colony	2054	IB annexes Sudan; JP reelected for life (at age 58)
Luna complains to the UN	2055	Holland is abandoned
Manhattan is abandoned	2056	Korean biotronic program exposed
PR Dugan killed at Far Point	2057	Universal Nanotech, Hyundai Shipyards
Dreadnought tragedy kills 312	2058	IB invades Ethiopia
First asteroid colony	2059	South Korean president assassinated
April 1 - Luna Independence Day	2060	North and South Korea become one
IB establishes Al Fahad on Luna	2061	Reformationists restrict Earthnet
Tokyo abandoned/Calconn Disaster	2062	Federation's Great Revival begins
Lunarian Treaty of Independence	2063	Rising sea levels top 9 meters
Al Fahad population passes 10,000	2064	Farcain establishes the Home Guard
Paradise asteroid swings past Earth	2065	World drought kills tens of millions
Hampton Bay collapse	2066	Scientific research stops in NAF

Historical Detail	Year	Historical Detail
First fusion plant operational	2067	IB annexes Libya and Algeria
Republic establishes Summerhaven	2068	Riots in Mexico kill hundreds
Trans Lunar Highway completed	2069	NAF rejects UN assistance
Tau Ceti probe begins its journey	2070	Turkey withdraws EU, joins IB
Martian microbial worms discovered	2071	NAF opens first reeducation camp
Tempel Dugan 10/31/72	2072	Rising sea levels top 13 meters
Luna's genetic program exposed	2073	Korea allies with IB
Religious radicals call for Luna's death	2074	Ivory Coast pirates seize EU ship
Republic establishes Prattville	2075	Canada votes to withdraw from the NAF
Luna Councilor Chi Lin assassinated	2076	US/Canada 10 Day War kills 1100
Cardinals win Super Bowl	2077	NAF declares martial law
Republic establishes Scottsbluff	2078	Water shortages across Middle East
ISS Shakti discovers life on Titan	2079	IB declares war on India (Food war)
Bombings begin all across Luna	2080	Rising sea levels top 17 meters
First bomb destroys a Lunarian farm (0)	2081	China allies with IB against India
Abby survives assassination attempt	2082	Australian government collapses
3 bombings in Shennong (19)	2083	Imam Bakr arrives buys SMT
Mine sabotage in Darpur (3)	2084	Kahfah Road completed
6 bombs, June 15, Black Friday (255)	2085	Incident at Salvation Rock
1st Highland convoy hijacked (6)	2086	Al Fahad exceeds 250,000
3 bombings during the year (26)	2087	SMT begins modifying convoys
Prattville water reservoir poisoned	2088	Pres. John Paul declares marshal law
7 bombings during the year (102)	2089	World refugees top 1 billion
2 bombings during the year (12)	2090	Rising sea levels top 20 meters
3 bombings during the year (46)	2091	Kashmir Agreement ends India war
4 bombings (39) and LCH (451)	2092	Al Fahad exceeds 500,000

	NAF President	Term
44	George Bush	2000-2008
45	Barack Obama	2008-2016
46	Elizabeth Ann Warren	2016-2024
47	Jesus Martinez	2024-2032
48	George Farcain	2032-2037
49	John Paul	2037-current

Lagrange Points

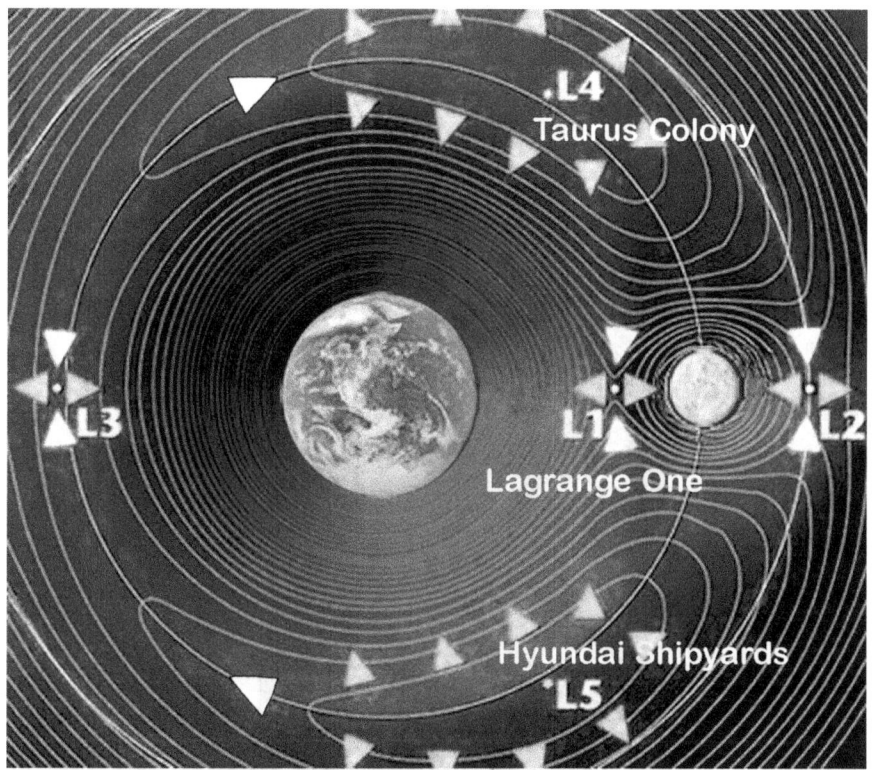

Lagrange Points are the gravitational eddies around any two massive objects such as the Earth and Luna. There are five positions in space where a third body, of comparatively negligible mass, can be placed which would then maintain its position relative to the two massive bodies. The gravitational fields of the two massive bodies combined with the centrifugal force are in balance at the Lagrange Points, allowing a third body to remain stationary with respect to the first two bodies. They all lie on the Earth/Luna orbital plane and share the same period as the moon. L1, L2, and L3 are quasi-stable and require station keeping to maintain long-term occupation. L4 and L5 are stable regions that naturally entrap dust and other small bodies.

Book 3: Evolution's Child – Thread

"Today is the Child of Tomorrow. We are all Evolution's Children Adrift on the Sea of Time."

Magi

Shennong

"And the four angels were loosed, which were prepared for an
hour, and a day, and a month, and a year,
for to slay the third part of men."

Holy Bible, Revelations 9:15

A thousand kilometers south of Aldrin Station, Shennong lies in the rim of Tycho Crater. With a population over six-hundred-thousand, it's the largest city in the Republic.

1

The Brotherhood's attack caught its citizens by surprise. Within hours, the invaders penetrate deep, keeping to the commonways, not even attempting to extend their control into the numerous avenues or nearby warrens. Instead, they seal every opening as they pass.

Security Chief Chen estimates they're facing over thirty thousand soldiers with thousands more outside on the surface. This is far too few to take Shennong by force. It's only a matter of time before Chen counterattacks and overwhelms the invaders.

Yangtze Commonway, like many others found throughout the Republic, is a giant passageway cut through the heart of Tycho's rim mountain. Filled with thousands of trees and other plants, it's part of a forest that serves the city as both air purifier and parkland.

Here, in this particular section of the commonway, the trees had been fifty-year old Sycamore's towering sixty meters in height. All that remains of these majestic plants are piles of blackened wood. The smoke of their burning obscures the distance, as if a fog were rolling in off a distant sea.

With the grace and power of a cheetah, Sergeant Lin Kai leaps over the body paying it no attention. Spread out behind him is the remnants of Shennong's 10th Metro Division. Of the twenty-two police officers in his own platoon, he's the last. Others have told him he should fall back, but nothing will compel Lin to give up the fight.

The intense beams sear through the smoke filled air of the commonway. The thunder of their passage echoes along the great corridor. The Brotherhood burns everything in their path, defocusing their beams to set whole groves of trees on fire. They're trying everything to slow down the incessant hit and run attacks the Lunarians have thrown at them.

Lin uses the trunk of one of these fallen giants to mask his approach. Timing his leap with the arrival of his comrades, he vaults over the tree and begins firing his disrupter and launching missiles. His fellow warriors follow him, laying down a withering fire on the convoys that lay a few hundred meters beyond.

Some of the big vehicles lumber about in an effort to bring more weapons to bear. Others stop, disgorging soldiers like ants swarming from their hole to face their attackers.

The Lunarians concentrate on the third Goliath. Missiles streak to their mark and penetrate the juggernaut. In a mighty explosion, its side rips open, flames shoot out and it grinds to a stop. Both of the tires on the left side collapse and it tips over. Black smoke billows from it and more explosions rock it, the last a massive detonation that causes the vehicles around it to scurry away.

The troop carrier directly behind the burning Goliath, itself full of holes and at least three missile strikes, catches fire and within moments, is a towering inferno. No one inside survives. The other carriers, further back, open their doors and soldiers pour out, eager to escape certain death. The undamaged troop carriers detach and look for another convoy.

Narrow beams of intense energy slice through the blinding smoke seeking victims. Brotherhood soldiers fall and die on a world not of their birth.

The Lunarians suffer as well. The warrior ten meters to Lin's left takes a beam to the chest and slumps to the ground, momentum lodging his lifeless body against the trunk of a fallen Sycamore. Another warrior has her arm removed at the elbow as she leaps over a tree trunk. She retreats to the waiting medics, her life spared by medical science to fight another day.

The skirmish is over in seconds. The convoys have completed their response maneuver and are dishing out energy on a scale that Lin's warriors cannot survive for long. However, they have accomplished what they set out to do and disappear back along the passageway, out of reach of the Brotherhood's weapons.

In the beginning, the Brotherhood sent soldiers after the retreating

3

Lunarians but when few returned, they stopped. Better to stay together and defend from a position of strength.

Chen feeds the illusion that there is strength in numbers while chipping away at the invaders. She's finally in a position to order a massive counterattack but hesitates knowing that casualties will be high. Better to wait and continue harassing them. A few days of sleep deprivation will soften the enemy and then she can strike.

Reaching some predetermined location, the Brotherhood turns off their incessant jammers and broadcasts their ultimatum on all frequencies.

"Cease all hostilities or your city will be destroyed. Our forces carry thermonuclear weapons which they will use unless you immediately comply." The message endlessly repeats.

With the network functioning again, Chen performs a security analysis of the situation. *Damn.* There are Brotherhood garrisons at the center of all fourteen boroughs. If they all have bombs then they have the ability to completely destroy her city but only if they are willing to commit suicide themselves. Why bring tens of thousands of soldiers along and all that hardware if all they wanted to do was blow the place up. The Brotherhood was after something and she needed to find out what.

Chen didn't doubt for a moment the existence of the deadly devices, she is well aware of the nukes her people found on the Sea of Clouds. After speed viewing the available vid records for the third time and consulting with her staff, she orders all front line warriors to disengage and fall back until further notice. *So… what is their plan? They hold my city hostage for what purpose?*

ЯL

Security Chief Chen didn't like what she had to do. "I'm not asking you to surrender. Simply back off until I can determine a course of action,"

"But Chief, we must drive them from Shennong." Sergeant Kai argues.

"Ask yourself why they have deliberately put themselves in such a precarious position? We will not risk a nuclear suicide bomb. Do I make myself clear?" She hates needing to be so firm with him. The young man's blood stained ghost suit attests to what he's gone through. His comrades are all dead and the handful of warriors he commands are remnants of other platoons. "I want you to fall back and let someone else take the lead. You have done everything possible under the circumstances."

"Chief, I want to finish this." Lin replies.

"Lin, we're not done here. Get your people some food and rest, and let me worry about the Brotherhood. That's an order." Chen can't afford to spend any more time with the young man. Waiting for his nod, she shifts her attention to another unit disengaging from the enemy. She's worried someone somewhere will take it upon themselves to continue the attack.

"Come on Lin. I could use some chow and a hot shower," Meili said. She and Luka are all that remains of Manchu platoon.

Lin looks around. He feels like a failure, that somehow he personally was to blame for the Brotherhood destroying Yangtze Commonway.

They had been in the middle of their attack run when the order to disengage came and the warriors had not retreated very far down the devastated commonway. It broke his heart to see the forest he played in as a boy in ruins. Smoke fills the great corridor making it difficult to see even using his sensors.

The beam strikes Meili in the upper torso at the base of her neck, effectively cutting off her head. Lin roars in anger and springs away. What remains of his ragtag unit scatters among the wreckage of the commonway, leaving behind more Lunarian blood to soak into the black dirt. Only Lin turns back, no longer caring if he lives or dies.

5

The young Lunarian keeps low and circles, staying hidden within the tangle of fallen trees. He sees the soldiers, their backs to him, their mission accomplished. He counts twenty-nine in this little group.

He checks his supply of missiles. He has only four remaining. Disrupter is running low but he could not have stopped even if it were empty.

The man last in line is the only one bothering to look back and then, only every other step or so. He never sees the shadow stalking them. Lin is within forty meters when he opens fire, spacing his shots, making every one count. The sound of his attack echoes down the great corridor causing the others in the group to scramble for cover. Before they do, the young Lunarian has killed six.

Beyond them, Lin can see the convoys that brought these men here. Without a second thought, he sends his last four missiles streaking towards the vehicles, one to the left, one to the right, and the final two targeting the center Goliath. The explosions rock the commonway.

He leaps over a pile of smoldering debris and kills another invader, and another. His missiles had not destroyed the convoys fighting ability and their powerful disrupters open up on Lin. Beams blister the air around him as he twists and turns, striving to keep something between him and certain death. He never senses the beam that gets him. One second he's fighting, the next his lifeless body is skidding to a stop. His unseeing eyes gaze upon eternity, another sacrifice on the altar of war.

ЯL

Inside his command center, Major Abdul Aziz is barely conscious. The twin blasts from the missiles has killed all of his senior staff. Blood is everywhere. They had been together as the announcement was given that all hostilities should cease immediately, anticipating complete capitulation. A squawking alarm testifies to the grave condition within the other two convoys. His command is in shambles.

He struggles to pull himself to a sitting position, pain lancing through his body. Gasping for breath, he looks down to see his chest covered in blood. Knowing his duty, he drags himself across the shattered interior of the vehicle. Moaning with every move, he takes the key from around his neck, inserts it into the console, and turns it. A red light flashes on.

Aziz swoons, barely staying conscious. He doesn't have much time. Laying a bloody hand on the palm reader, he said, *"Emergency Override Code Major Abdul Aziz. Zero one zero six six six zero."*

"Authorization accepted and countdown begun," the computerized male voice said in the same language, the last words he will hear in his beloved native tongue.

"Allah Akbar," the Major puts his back to the console as the loss of blood and pain finally takes its toll. He's at peace with his god, knowing he's performed his duties to the best of his ability. He welcomes death, seeing it only as a transformation from the hardships of this life to the promised paradise in the next.

Word spreads fast of the imminent detonation. The various commanders issued orders for their soldiers to take cover as soon as the news arrived. This is an event they have all anticipated, when one of their units would find it necessary to perform the ultimate sacrifice.

"Allah Akbar," the Major chants. His thoughts turn to his family and the things he regrets. He assures himself that all will be forgiven because of his service to Allah. Beating his wives and children had been necessary and lawful under Islamic Law. The only regret that eats at his heart is the death of his daughter. Her stubborn disobedience was intolerable but her death had made all his other children respect his subsequent decisions. Now, at the instant of his own demise, all he can see are her young eyes staring accusingly at him as the villagers stoned her.

Groaning with intense pain, in the final few seconds of his life the Major leans forward and touches his forehead to the cold metal floor, a position promising the comfort of long use.

The nuke detonates forming a tiny sun in the heart of Shennong. The sheer size of Yangtze Commonway isn't sufficient to route the energy away from the surrounding habitats. The core of the detonation is a ravenous shockwave that pulses through the mountain causing the free surfaces of the underground metropolis to explode, showering the spaces within with huge chunks of rock. The blast sends a massive firestorm down the great passageway following the path of least resistance. It engulfs everything until it reaches the cities Eastern Access Tunnel. The mighty airlocks, damaged by the passing shockwave, cannot hold. The nuclear fire blows them open and races down the city's main access tunnel, emerging from the mountain and venting its fire to space. By this time, the center of the blast has carved out a cavity almost a kilometer in diameter, weakening the mountain.

With a major commonway open to vacuum, the wind reaches gale force as the cities atmosphere spews into space. Outside, the air and debris form a fog that gathers over the stricken city.

Most Brotherhood units had sufficient warning of the impending blast to reach the safety of their troop carriers. Even so, the detachment nearest to Linchuan suffers the brunt of the blast. The fierce nuclear fire and shockwave rips through their carriers, tossing them like children's toys. Of the four convoys and over two thousand men, no one survives.

Farther away, the Brotherhood's heavy vehicles weather the storm. Hunkered down inside their Goliaths and troop carriers, the pressure wave passes over them without harm.

Lunarians caught in the open are not so lucky. The tremendous shock wave, focused by the enormous stone corridor, crushes them like bugs.

As the fury of the blast spends itself, the weakened mountain collapses, sinking into the cavity that Allah's fire has carved. A huge cloud of dust and gas rises above the sinkhole for thousands of meters fed by the death of a hundred habitats. They implode under the shifting mass of rock, explosively releasing their air to space.

One sixth of the city is gone. One-hundred-thousand citizens are dead or dying. Survivors struggle to put aside their shock and horror and try to save what they can. They abandon Shennong.

Scottsbluff

"A man by himself is in bad company."

Eric Hoffer (1902-1983)

Cris hides his bike amidst some rocks and moves carefully the last few feet to peek down at Hallstead. Nothing much appears to have changed. The Goliath is still there but no rovers. The two missing rovers are lying in ruins at the bottom of a cliff several kilometers away. They'll not be killing any more Lunarians.

Where is everyone? Cris pinpoints six sentries but otherwise, nothing moves. *Only six?* Cris angers as though slapped in the face. The Brotherhood commander's not taking him seriously even after losing four rovers, a decision he will soon regret.

Cris creeps over the edge, stealthily making his way into the encampment. He times his moves with those of the guards and lays a trap at the rear of the last carrier.

As the soldier turns the corner, he walks onto the Highlander's sword. Starting low and aiming high, Cris drives the thin blade between the layered ceramic plates. It takes all of his considerable strength to penetrate the underlying puncture resistant material, and all of his skill

10

to keep the convulsing body from snapping the blade at the hilt. The metal sings as it slides past the hard plates, sending a strange tone up his arm to his ears, the swan song of a man dying far from home. The sound is expected but disconcerting.

His aim is true, slicing through the heart, killing instantly. Cris eases the body to the ground, sliding his sword out with care. This sound is different, like a baby's weak cry. Cris steels himself to finish the job. He wipes the sword on the arm of his victim then rolls the body under the carrier. The dead man's blood boils in the vacuum. He must hurry before it draws attention.

Cris moves to the airlock and enters. Sword in one hand and disrupter in the other, he watches the inner door cycle open. Just out of sight to his right, the Highlander's visor picks up heavy breathing and elevated heartbeats. Stepping boldly from the airlock, he confronts two men in shirtsleeves sitting at a table only a few meters away. They are both looking at him as if they have seen a ghost.

For a split second, nobody moves. Then all hell breaks loose.

One soldier shouts something unintelligible and reaches for the pistol holstered at his waist. Cris shoots him in the chest as he leaps across the intervening distance, the sound thunderous in the enclosed space. With one swipe of his blade, Cris cuts the other man's throat, almost severing his head in the process. Blood fountains from the gaping wound, the look of shocked disbelief frozen on the face. The bodies hit the floor almost simultaneously.

Cris scans the inside of the troop carrier. He's alone. In both directions are narrow bunks stacked from floor to ceiling. A quick count reveals enough for at least fifty soldiers and their gear. If all ten carriers were the same, that put this contingent at about five-hundred soldiers.

Lockers at each end of the carrier draws his attention. Opening one, he finds a wealth of ordnance, everything from missiles to land mines. This is what he came for. Cris fills two large bags. Before he leaves, he sets a timer on one of the remaining charges and closes the locker.

Exiting the transport, Cris slips down the length of the convoy placing explosives under each carrier. Last, he attaches several ounces of SuperX on the Goliaths undercarriage near its fuel cell supply tanks, setting its timer to go off first. Along the way, he makes some interesting observations concerning the carrier modifications, things that will come in handy later. Sergeant Cristobal Calatrava did all of this without any of the remaining guards seeing him, a shadow in the night.

Cris returns to his bike and secures the bulging bags. Gunning the machine, he races down the ravine away from Hallstead. Moments later, he stops near the summit of a nearby hill looking down on the compound.

Brotherhood soldiers are swarming around the convoy like a bunch of ants. One of them, crawling along on his knees, spots the device planted on the Goliath and begins waving his arms and pointing. Another bugeye comes running up and squirms on his back under the massive vehicle just as the device explodes. The charge ruptures the hyperbolic fuel tanks and violently mixes their contents. The resulting fireball engulfs the Goliath. It disintegrates into a million pieces. Chunks of aluminum and titanium shred the soldiers around it and rips open the nearest carrier.

The debris was just beginning to settle when the other charges begin going off. In complete silence, all ten troop carriers explode, one after the other. Dust, gasses and human body fluids gather above the convoy in a thick blanket. With no wind to carry it away, dissipation takes time. Dead and wounded are scattered everywhere.

Secondary explosions rock what remains of the convoy as Cris turns away, his anger sated for the moment. Survivors will speak of a demon with a sword, a ghost with teeth.

𝕽𝕷

For hours, Lazarus has soared alone above an endless lunar landscape, the omnipresent face of Earth his only companion. The airless world of Luna scrolls by thirty meters below. His visor filters out the Moonhawks and all they contain. Even when he looks down at himself, he sees only the stark inhospitable lunar terrain sailing past. Lazarus is a solitary spirit in a vast wilderness.

The battle of Nell's Valley is vivid in his mind and he struggles against rising panic. He may not believe in heaven, but he just witnessed hell. Mortal combat is as close to hell as humanity can devise, brutality unchecked by the slightest hint of compassion.

He linked with Lindsey right before the fight started. It lasted only a couple of minutes, but in those minutes, his life changed. Lazarus no longer holds any remnant of belief that war contains glory. War is death, blatant and brutal.

Lindsey had overlaid all twelve warriors into a single point of view. The composite was unimaginably violent. Fully immersed in the experience, Lazarus witnessed the massacre of scores of Brotherhood soldiers, their deaths thrust upon him through the eyes of the slayer. It's worse because it's his first total immersion. Like an addict taking their first injection, it hits him hard. Each death sent shockwaves through him, hearing, seeing, smelling, and feeling the battle as though he were the killer. The explosions, the blood red fog erupting from their wounds, and worst of all, the deaths of Brice and Kitajima. He felt the beams cut through their bodies, hear their last gasp, feel their life drain from them.

After Kitajima died, Lindsey severed his link with Quan Kiai and pushed him to take control of the cannon. And he did. He blasted away at the Brotherhood racking up two confirmed kills and many more in the frigate. He had never killed before.

13

He shudders, clenching his eyes tightly shut. Through it all, Tempel, Sam and the others are running around like animals. *What have I done?* Panic crowds his mind. *Why did I come here?*

Like father, like son. He grabs at his father's memory like a lifeline but it can't contain the fear. It builds to the point that spots dance before his eyes. The very idea of people that are not people frightens him to his core. Is it possible that what the Federation said about the Lunarians is true? *Are they animal mutants?* He can't shake the thought that, for all their kindness and beauty, they're not human. His head spins. The harder he tries to make sense of the situation, the worse it becomes.

"Lazarus?" Lindsey calls softly as if from a great distance.

"I've given him a neuro-cognitive. He should be fine." Doc Grady said, also dim and distant.

Lazarus struggles against the descending darkness, clawing his way towards the voices. Someone begins massaging his shoulders whispering softly in his ear.

"*Relax… take deep breaths…* That's better. You had me worried there for a moment," Lindsey said, continuing to administer to him. She has linked and readjusted his visual. He's no longer alone in the void.

"Take it easy… relax…" Lindsey's lips brush his ear while she works his shoulder muscles. "It's my fault, I should not have let you immerse in the battle. It was too much for a first time," Lindsey said continuing to massage his neck and shoulders.

Lazarus looks up. Her eyes are exquisite jewels looking back at him, her beautiful face framed once again with raven black hair and the same form-fitting sky-blue blouse as when they first met, all courtesy of the processing capabilities of their linked visors.

"Welcome back," she said smiling.

"Are you one of them?" He asked.

"What do you mean, one of them? Are you referring to the Lunarians? Or to Quan Kiai?" She keeps the edge out of her voice. Now's not the time to rail on Lazarus for being an insensitive boob.

"Is there a difference?" Lazarus asks, recalling their beastly four-legged sprint. His fear stirs.

"Yes, there's a difference."

"Are they designed for war?" his tone of voice lays a heavy-handed verdict upon the very idea.

"Look, just because they're different, doesn't make them evil," Lindsey said. "I've lived with them their entire life and I assure you, they love and laugh just like you do. Where's your fear truly coming from? Is it because of what they are or is it what they did?"

"They kill so... effortlessly," Lazarus said.

"You mistake efficiency for enthusiasm. These men and women did what needed doing. War is not something you pussyfoot around with," Lindsey said.

"Using genetic science to maintain health is one thing, using it to create better soldiers is something else. How can you justify this perversion?" Lazarus asks.

"Tempel's not a perversion. Sam's not a perversion. You're not thinking like the man I sponsored for citizenship. This is the Federation talking..." she stares at him for a moment. "Come with me," she loosens his restraining harness and pulls him to his feet. They go back several rows. Zoey is on one side of the aisle. Another warrior is on the other side, Marcel Piqualow. They're both asleep.

His visor shows Zoey and Marcel as they would appear without their ghost suits dressed in normal attire. The young woman looks so... peaceful. It's hard to imagine her as the brutal killer he witnessed during the battle.

"What's wrong with her?" Lazarus looks down at Zoey.

"Doc said they're suffering from battle fatigue. They're having problems dealing with what happened in Nell's Valley... War is not something any sane person yearns for but when one society inflicts it upon another… someone must answer the call. We asked Zoey and Marcel to do a horrible thing and they did it. Can we now condemn them for doing what we asked them to do?" Lindsey shakes her head, "No… the Republic must thank them for what they did and take care of them, no matter what."

Lazarus recalls the kindness Zoey had shown him during his vacsuit training. Fear slips away and concern takes its place. After all, it's not as if they had killed innocent people. They had killed his lifelong enemy.

Unbeknownst to Lazarus, he reaches these conclusions with help from Doc Grady's drugs. They dull his memories allowing him to temper the brutality of the killing with ignorance, just as he would have done if he had not experienced the slaughter in the first place. The battle fades and the genetic engineering seem less important. As his attitude improves, he feels better and more like his old self.

"Will they be all right?" Lazarus asks.

"Doc said yes but nothing's for certain," Lindsey replies.

"Is there anything I can do?"

Lindsey shakes her head, "Let them rest in peace…"

ℛ𝕃

Jamie shakes his head "The attack severely segmented Magi. Until we reestablish the network, Magi will not be Magi."

"Unacceptable. I need Magi," Corso said.

"You'll have her. We rebooted part of the system. Magi should be coming up momentarily," Jamie said.

"We adjusted some of the emotion control programs within the Grokian Interface which should act like a sedative. But Jamie's right, until Magi's whole, she will be different," Jordan said.

"Different how?" Corso asks.

"So many have died… I have failed…" Magi whimpers.

"Magi." Corso exclaims. It looks like Magi but without the twinkle in her eye or the ready smile. Her hair is almost fully gray and she looks much older. Sadness and defeat lay heavy upon her.

"I've informed the families of the deaths of their loved ones. The pain I've caused is incalculable. I'm so sorry Corso. I have failed."

"Magi. That's absolutely wrong." Corso exclaims. "You are NOT responsible for their deaths or the pain inflicted on their families. Without you, we don't stand a chance, so unless you want more people to die, you need to start helping me stop this."

"I'm at reduced capacity," Magi states flatly. "You should not trust my judgment."

"How many threads are you processing with?" Corso asks.

"Less than three hundred thousand," the AI said. "Nothing outside of Aldrin Station."

"It will have to do," Corso said.

"Magi hasn't operated with that low a thread count since the late fifties," Jordan said.

"We'll get some relays on top of Rim Mountain to reestablish the link with New London, Prattville, and Summerhaven. That'll bring in another hundred-fifty thousand threads. In the meantime, I want the precise location of the nukes the Brotherhood claim to be carrying."

"The data is incomplete. I can't be sure of anything," Magi claims.

"I know. Just give me your best estimate," Corso pleads.

"Corso... If I'm wrong..."

"The final decision's mine," Corso said. Magi turns away. "Magi... Aldrin Station can't survive with the Brotherhood in our commonways. We must destroy their nukes and evict these invaders."

"I've determined when the devices arrived. They were flown in right before the attack began, during the time that Councilor Taylor rescinded your order halting all incoming flights." Magi can't look at Corso.

"Put together a summary and submit it to the General Council for arbitration. I will deal with this when there's time. Where are the nukes now?"

"The probability of the nukes being in this specific location is only at 59%," Magi said, turning back to Corso, tears streaming down her face.

Corso has never seen Magi cry before but he doesn't have time right now to deal with anything except staying alive. "Keep working on it. Send some spybots in for a look."

An explosion, much louder and closer than those before, rings the RCC like a bell. The lights flash once and the Command Center goes dark.

"Ben. Report." Corso orders. Dim emergency lights come on. Everyone stares at the huge airlock door as if it were about to open. Fear and tension permeates the assembly. No one moves.

"The RCC is under attack. Mini rockets have breached the outer perimeter and are being met by the guards," Ben said.

"They're being overwhelmed. The numbers of minis coming at them is staggering." Magi said sadly. "They've lost half their number already."

"Form up." Ben steps forward. Security's his job. He wonders briefly how the attackers had managed to get by the many layers of sensors guarding the RCC but now's not the time to think, it's time to act. "Move it." he shouts as he paces back and forth in front of the airlock door, cradling a disrupter in the crook of his arm. His troops gather their weapons and prepare for battle. He senses in them both fear and anxiety but no hesitation. They'll fight.

Ben looks over the company. "Listen up. We do this by the book. When the airlock opens, proceed at full speed. When we get to the upper chamber, spread out and attack in pairs. *Lock and Load.* It's time to take it to the enemy."

The heavy airlock door swings open and Ben leads them through.

ЯL

Hour after hour, the two Moonhawks maintain a course due east, passing Thebit Crater along its southern rim. They keep low and slow, never more than ten meters above the surface and under a hundred kilometers per hour. This ate into the remaining fuel.

The pace is stressful on the pilots. Without Magi, they can't rely on the resident AI to fly the ships on autopilot. Too many human decisions are needed while maneuvering across the broken landscape. Therefore, they divide the responsibility among the warriors, not asking anyone to fly for long.

Tempel begins scanning for emissions from the town long before they see the towering rim wall of Faye crater. The total lack of broadband chatter is ominous. He probes the ridge as they creep over the horizon. The arrays of satellite communications equipment that should be there is scattered down the mountainside.

Scottsbluff had a decent defensive shield in place before the attack. If part of that survived the bombardment, Quan Kiai could face a formidable weapon. They all have a great deal of respect for the big laser cannons his people designed and built in defense against the meteorites.

Tempel tags an LZ in a deep depression a few kilometers from Scottsbluff. The two Moonhawks come to rest a few meters apart. Corazon launches a spybot, landing it on a nearby ridge with a view of the settlement's main entrance. The instant it comes to rest, Tempel zooms in on the structures clustered outside the town's main gate.

The bombardment had been intense. Everything's crumpled and smashed. Craters pockmark the mountainside and out onto the plain. Twisted metal is all that remains of the sheds and warehouses outside Scottsbluff. Nothing moves. Even the vapor hanging over the wreckage seems frozen in place.

Tempel points the spybots communications laser towards the main gate, "Scottsbluff, how do you copy?" he said and waits.

The seconds tick by. Maybe no one's listening or maybe… everyone's dead.

"Scottsbluff, this is Senior Lieutenant Dugan of the Lincoln County Police Department. Please respond." Turning to Consuela, Tempel asks, "Are we transmitting on all frequencies?"

"Aye, they should be receiving full visual. They're not responding," Consuela replies.

"If they don't, someone will need to go in and find out why." Tempel doesn't like the sound of that but sees no alternative.

From somewhere near the base of the mountain, a low wattage broadband laser comes to life. "What do you want?" No image accompanies the question but the voice is female, familiar, and frightened.

With a sigh of relief, Tempel said, "Magi? Is that you?"

"Who are you? How do you know my name?"

"Lieutenant Tempel Dugan from Aldrin Station."

"Aldrin Station?" The frightened voice takes on a wistful quality as though remembering something lost.

From near Scottsbluff's main entrance, a second more tightly focused communication laser links with the spybot. The signal strength increases as data begins to flow both ways. An older man appears before them. Gray stubble and heavy dark circles under his eyes betray fatigue.

"Security Chief Gordon O'Leary… Who did you say you are?" After the last few days, he's not sure whom to trust.

From the database on board the Moonhawks, they know a lot about Scottsbluff including its Chief of Security. He's a relatively new Lunarian having arrived a mere thirty-three years earlier. Born in Ireland, he grew up in the small hamlet of Graystones just south of Dublin. For centuries, the historic fishing village looked out on the Irish Sea. However, thirty-three years ago, rising sea levels forced everyone out, an event that prompted Gordon O'Leary to emigrate to the moon.

"Greetings Chief O'Leary. I'm Lieutenant Tempel Dugan."

The image of a man and a woman appear next to O'Leary. Each consists of some three thousand villagers, separated by gender, then morphed into a single entity. From this agglomeration, a middle-aged man emerges and asks, "What the hell's happening?"

This is unusual. Seldom do observers take part in conversations.

Tempel turns to his questioner, "The Republic is under attack. Beyond that, I would feel better if we were face to face for any further discussion."

The female image morphs into an older woman. "You must do better than that Lieutenant," she declares, a double breach of etiquette. "What was your mission and why can't you return to Aldrin Station?"

"While on official Republic business we were attacked by the Brotherhood. We lost four. I'll provide access to the vids as soon as we're inside Scottsbluff. We need fuel and air," Tempel said.

The female image morphs into a teen girl, "I don't trust them. Send them on."

Turning to address the young woman, O'Leary said, "Margay, I'm sorry for your loss but we can't do that. When you're older, you'll understand. They're Lunarians. We must help them."

"I don't like it." Margay declares. The attack bloodied Scottsbluff and others, young and old, male and female, join her in expressing the same feeling of misgiving. Many are adamant about not becoming involved. They're frightened.

"Please, all of you, be reasonable. We must take them in. It's our duty as Lunarians," O'Leary pleads.

"Leary's right," a voice rises above the babble. "They're officers and citizens. They need air, for Pat's sake. We can't deny them air."

"We're involved whether you like it or not," another said.

"Max is right. You don't think they bombed us just for fun do you? The Brotherhood will be coming and we must be ready."

Someone posted a poll and within moments, the citizens of Scottsbluff reach a consensus, but it was close.

"The vote is cast and the majority has spoken. We let them in. It's the right thing to do," O'Leary said. Turning back to Tempel, "The main access tunnel is still passable. I'll meet you in the hanger."

$$\mathcal{RL}$$

Marcel struggles to throw off the fog that fills his mind. He opens his eyes. He's strapped to a seat in one of the Moonhawks. Doc Grady's standing in the aisle looking at him.

"Take it easy. You've been asleep for quite awhile." Doc said.

"How long?" Marcel asks. His mouth tastes like cotton.

"About nine hours," Doc replies.

"Nine hours. Where the hell are we?" Zoey asks from across the aisle.

"We're approaching Scottsbluff," Doc said.

"Why did you knock me out?" Marcel asks. Anger stirs.

"Because you were headed down a slippery slope and needed time to mend. Sometimes the best medicine is to let your body's natural healing processes work its magic over a nice long sleep cycle. What you're going through has been called many things down through the years, combat stress reaction, battle fatigue, or shell shock. Take your pick." Doc Grady said. "In a nutshell, your mind's rebelling against your actions, and the best treatment for it is sleep."

Doc Grady is treating him and Zoey for combat stress. As this sinks in and Marcel realizes the implications, his embarrassment quickly turns to concern. He's never been ill in his life, not even a runny nose. "What's wrong with me?" He asked.

"Nothing's wrong with you. Your psyche is adapting to war. Your reaction to the battle is understandable and predictable." Doc Grady pauses, "No one likes killing. If they did, we would start looking for a neurological abnormality or protein imbalance. You have had a completely normal reaction."

"So… have you given this little talk to the others?" Marcel asks.

"Everyone handles it in their own way. No two people are alike." Doc Grady said.

"The short answer is no." Marcel said. *Great. Just Great.*

"Hey, on the bright side, if you're going to take a ride on the crazy train, it's always good to have a friend along," Zoey said to him with a wicked grin. *Brice will find this amusing.* Her grin vanishes. Brice is dead.

Doc Grady sighs, "Neither of you are crazy, just human."

The badlands along the edge of the Sea of Clouds rise abruptly about fifty kilometers out of Al Fahad. Cris uses his disrupter to drill the last of thirty-five deep holes into the sheer mountainside, his vacsuit protecting him from the blow back. He pours a quantity of powdered SuperX into the hole then adds a detonator. The charges are scattered along a kilometer looking down on Kahfah Road.

Like a monkey in his favorite tree, Cris moves across the nearly vertical landscape with ease. This is his environment. He grew up exploring the rugged lunar landscape. Cris scrambles up the steep slope and settles down against a boulder to wait.

The roadbed glows in the starlight a hundred meters below. From where he sits, he can see who's coming all the way to the horizon back towards Al Fahad.

Cris doesn't have long to wait. The scouts are first, many kilometers ahead of the main body. He lets them pass unharmed.

Behind them is a column of Goliaths that do not pull any carriers. The massive vehicles bristle with heavy disrupter cannons. Cris has never seen anything like them. Their only discernible purpose is to destroy. He lets them pass as well.

Finally, the graders, compactors, and their support vehicles appear. These are the road and bridge builders, the Brotherhood's Corp of Engineers. Following them are troop convoys pulled by more of the heavily armed Goliaths. Convoys extend as far back as Cris can see. He shudders as he realizes the full extent of what's coming at Aldrin Station.

The trap is set and his targets are in the kill zone. It's time to slow this parade down.

Cris transmits the signal that detonates all thirty-five charges simultaneously. He feels the shock through his ass. Dust devils jet outward across the stricken mountainside. At first, nothing happens. Then the entire mass starts to slide downhill, slow at first, but gaining speed with each passing second.

The vehicles below are oblivious to the danger until thousands of tons of basalt crashes down, crushing them like a boot stepping on an ant. It's over in an instant.

The main column is in turmoil and Cris adds to it. He begins detonating the land mines he planted in the roadway, aiming for the Goliaths. The troop carriers are immobile without them.

The orderly procession has degenerated into outright confusion. This stretch of road passes through some of the worst terrain on Luna, a land of sheer cliffs and steep mountainsides, of fissures hundreds of meters deep and big enough to swallow a convoy. They cannot go forward and the road is only wide enough for a single truck to pass in many places. It will be hours, perhaps days, before they will regain control and without their Engineers, they cannot simply repair the road, they will need another route. He knows of only one, and it's his next stop.

Cris triggers the last landmine then turns his back on the hell he's created. The movement catches the eye of scanners below and shots begin to rain in around him. A few come close but he's too stealthy for the gunners to get a clear target, a shadow among shadows.

Before disappearing over the ridge, Cris gives them something to remember. He pulls his sword and briefly holds it aloft making its silhouette visible from below. Then he's gone.

ЯL

Before the Brotherhood attack, there had been a row of Quonset huts just outside the main entrance. Common all across Luna, the metal Quonset shades people working on the surface during the long lunar day. Only one still stands, heavily damaged and full of holes.

As they slip past, sensors probe its depths. Benches, tools, equipment, and a forklift lay broken on its floor. Trapped inside is a haze consisting mostly of oils and lubricants. A small but distinctive trace amount of blood and urine is also present. Someone died here.

"This place got hammered," Marcel murmurs.

"Let's keep our mind on what we're doing," Tempel said.

The Moonhawks glide towards the mouth of Scottsbluff's main gate. The corrugated metal extension outside the entrance is broken and battered but the airlock door itself appears undamaged. A sliver of light breaks the darkness when the giant door begins to open.

Moonhawk One leads the way into the tunnel. It felt good to have stone overhead once again. They pass through two more doors until finally emerging into the town's main hanger. The Moonhawk's thrusters whine loudly in the pressurized space, a welcome sound. Parked along one side of the vast room are a Goliath and several ore carriers. Numerous smaller vehicles, six wheeled transports, four wheeled rovers, two wheeled bikes, and the tools and supplies of a town lay scattered across

25

the expansive floor. Across the way, three people are waving their arms.

The thrusters echo in the closed space. The Moonhawks settle side by side before the three villagers. Silence descends once again.

"We're being denied access to their network," Consuela said.

"Marcel, Corazon, you're with me. Tatiana, keep everyone else in the ships. We don't want to be here long," Tempel said.

"Aye," they respond.

"Tempel, I think it's wise if I make first contact," Lindsey said. "Look at yourself. You're wearing a ghost suit. These people have never seen a ghost suit and probably don't know much about genetic modifications either. Scottsbluff's a community of Purists. If you walk out there like that, they may just change their mind about helping us."

Tempel suppresses the feed coming from Sam, seeing her as the villagers will see him, a featureless dark shadow in the shape of a person.

"They're Lunarians. However, I see your point... Fine, you go talk to the man," Tempel said.

Lindsey unbuckles as Tempel lowers the ramp. It's been a long mission and it's not over yet. She moves down the ramp and walks over to the people. Lazarus follows.

"Greetings Chief O'Leary, I'm Lindsey Marquest and this is Lazarus Sheffield."

"Greetings. This is Hugh Grimsby and his wife Amber. I was expecting Lieutenant Dugan?" Already the plan was changing. He didn't like it.

"He's inside. He sent me to prepare you for his unusual appearance."

"Unusual? What do you mean?"

"He and his platoon are wearing ghost suits."

"Ghost suits? Never heard of them. Is it something new?" Amber Grimsby asks. She's never been comfortable with Luna's rapidly evolving technology. One of the reasons she moved to Scottsbluff years ago was to escape the fast pace in Aldrin Station. Things just move slower out here.

"Yes, very new… If you will grant us access to your network you will be able to see Lieutenant Dugan instead of his ghost suit."

Under the hanger's bright lights, a persistent dark shadow is hard to miss, especially one that walks on its own. "Greetings Chief O'Leary," Tempel said, emerging from the ship.

All three villagers start backpedaling in alarm as the figure approaches. They have no idea what's confronting them and after the last few days, this is too much.

Lindsey steps forward raising her hands. "Take it easy. I apologize for the scare. You have nothing to fear." She moves to stand between them and the apparition. "Lieutenant Dugan is wearing a very special vacsuit, that's all. If you will grant visual access, I can prove it."

O'Leary stops. The strange blackness of the ghost suit swallows his vision but he knows what energy absorbent materials are and can reasonably assimilate what he's seeing with science. Gathering his wits, he said, "We don't normally treat visitors this way. Magi would have granted you access automatically. Joan, provide our visitors with level one access."

The ghost suit transforms into a handsome young man wearing the familiar black and gray uniform of a police officer.

"Chief O'Leary, this is Lieutenant Tempel Dugan," Lindsey said.

"Greetings. This is Hugh and Amber Grimsby."

Hugh Grimsby is short and slim with straight brown hair pulled back in a ponytail. He's conservative and distrusts change.

Amber Grimsby is several centimeters taller with short black hair barely covering the tops of her ears. She looks worried and a little shell-shocked.

"Why have you come here?" Amber asks. There's more than fear inside this woman, there's strength as well.

"We had no choice. The Republic is under attack and we need

supplies," Tempel said.

Amber shrugs. "So what? It's not our fight. Aldrin Station is four hundred kilometers away. We want to stay out of it."

"The Brotherhood won't let you stay out of it." Lazarus said.

"You know this for a fact?" Hugh asks.

Lazarus looks intently at the young man. "They bombed you."

"Maybe that was a warning to stay out of it." Hugh said.

Lazarus shrugs, "You're Lunarians. The Brotherhood believes it's their duty to bring you into the way of Allah. So unless you're willing to live under Islamic law, you're in this fight whether you like it or not."

Tempel's link-monitor flashes as the number climbs. Already in the thousands, it marks the pace at which the citizens of Scottsbluff are downloading the vid from Nell's Valley. At this rate, it will only be a matter of moments before they will know far more than they bargained for.

Tempel turns to the older man. "Chief O'Leary, can we get fuel and air lines started. It's best if we are out of here quickly."

The older man nods. "Hugh, can you see to that?"

"Marcel, Corazon, help him," Tempel said. "Thanks Chief. From the looks of things, they hit Scottsbluff hard."

"Please, call me Leary…" he sighs and for a moment, looks much older than his years, "Twelve hours ago we lost our network link with the rest of the Republic. We still had our sensors and could see that every last satellite had been blown to bits including Lagrange One."

Tempel nods.

"Then the bombs came. Before we knew what was going on, fourteen people died," Leary said wearily, "including our First Responders."

Tempel nods again. He figured as much. "The Brotherhood must have been planning this for years."

"Planning what? What's this mean?" Amber asks. She was among the first to finish reviewing the events of Nell's Valley.

Tempel said, "It means we're at war. The Brotherhood has every intention of becoming humanity's first multi-planet empire."

"You don't say." Leary exclaims.

More and more people converge on the hanger, crowding forward to gather around Quan Kiai. A murmur starts that rapidly grows as they realize the implications of what they had just seen.

"They have brought nuclear weapons into Scottsbluff."

"We don't want anything to do with genetic engineering."

"There not Pure. Send them away."

"We moved out here to get away from all the genetics practiced in the city."

"A child should be the product of a single man and woman, not a bunch of gene splicing and other mucky muck."

The protest grows louder by the second.

"Here. Here. What's this about nuclear weapons?" Chief O'Leary asks turning to Tempel.

"We recovered nukes from a crash site out on the Sea of Clouds. Review the vid," Tempel looks over the crowd. He spreads his hands wide, palms up, and said. "As soon as we refuel we'll go."

"They're not Pure. These young folks have had their genetics all mangled up. They're not human."

"Look, Tempel and Quan Kiai are defending your right to practice your beliefs as you see fit. Having us here for a few minutes won't contaminate you." Lindsey said rather bluntly. She's losing patience.

O'Leary finishes viewing the battle at Nell's Valley and turns to Tempel. "What are you people?"

"Sam, can you come out here?" Tempel asks.

Hundreds of villagers have gathered in the hanger. They form a solid mass around Quan Kiai. Tempel looks at the faces around him and motions for Sam to remove her headgear. She releases the molyseal along her jaw line, pulls the breathing unit from her face, and peels it over her head letting it hang behind her like a hood. She keeps her visor on.

"This is Sergeant Samantha Odegaard. You needn't be frightened of her or any of us. We're police officers sworn to protect you," Tempel said.

"Just as you have all benefited from genetic science, so have we, only in us, it's been taken a step further. Don't let this frighten you. We're just as human as you are," Sam said.

The crowd is restless, unconvinced, staring at the strangers with suspicion. After what's happened, this is almost beyond their comprehension. From somewhere near the back comes a voice, "We just want to be left alone."

"Aye, we don't need these freaks."

"These are our best young men and women. They're not freaks." Lindsey said.

From somewhere else in the crowd, "Well, she isn't pure human, is she? No one who moves like that is pure human."

"Tempel, if I may," Sam said.

When Tempel turns, she's already opened the ghost suits front molyseal and her intentions are clear.

"Go for it Sam," Tempel said.

With Tempel helping, she peels off the vacsuit. Sam stands before them in only a thin garment covering her genitals. Moments later, even this lies on the hanger floor. She's completely nude.

Without exception, she has the attention of the entire village. She spreads her arms and turns letting them see her at all angles.

The people murmur nervously.

"She's definitely a woman." a man said from the crowd.

"What about the guys?" a woman asks.

Tempel immediately begins to strip. With Sam's help, he's soon standing nude beside her. They walk hand in hand among the villagers who part like the Red Sea during the exodus.

"Can you show us how you run on all fours?"

In response, Tempel flexes his knees, leans forward, bare feet gripping the stone floor, and leaps. The crowd scrambles to get out of his way. At the end of the arc, he reaches out with well muscled arms and propels himself forward, using his upper body strength to coil his legs beneath him and push. The young warrior bounds around the hanger taking his time but giving a good show. The villagers marvel at his grace and fluidity. They murmur excitedly and step back as Tempel returns. They oh and ah when he finishes the little demonstration by smoothly resuming bipedal motion. Tatiana is helping Sam put her ghost suit back on and Angel steps up to help Tempel.

"It's not natural." a villager said.

"We came out here to escape such things," another said.

"You can ignore progress, but you can't escape it. Sooner or later it will find you and thrust itself into your lives," Lindsey said.

"Lieutenant, the ships are fueled and stocked," Marcel reports.

Tempel, only partly back in his ghost suit, said to Chief O'Leary. "We'll reestablish the network as soon as possible, and I'll let Corso know how helpful you've been. Look, if the Brotherhood shows up, don't try fighting them. Run and hide."

Chief O'Leary frowns, "Don't worry about us. We'll be fine."

The Preacher

"No, I don't know that atheists should be considered as citizens, nor should they be considered as patriots. This is one nation under God."

George H.W. Bush (1924-?)

The chamber's a man's room with dark wood paneling and darker furniture. A long mahogany conference table dominates the room. Recessed ceiling lamps cast bright pools of light on its polished surface.

The tension around the table is palpable. The Federation's top brass are waiting for their Commander-in-Chief. They must inform him of dire events.

Without warning, two marines swing open the big double doors.

President John Paul sweeps into the room. The tall gangling figure of Reverend Gibson is at his side and a covey of young interns at their heels. Chairs slide back from the table, muffled by the heavy carpet. The officers rise to their feet.

"Attention." Major General Thomas Fitzpatrick calls out. He's many decades past his prime, bone white hair and muscles sagging under the weight of years. However, he bleeds Army green, having worked his way up from the enlisted ranks during a distinguished forty-five year career, the last eleven as Chief of Staff.

"As you were gentlemen," President John Paul said. He and Reverend Gibson take the seats reserved for them. They are at the midpoint of the table, facing the giant vid screen. The rest of the entourage settles into chairs lining the wall behind their boss. Prior administrations would not have dared bring these lackeys into the inner sanctum of the White House Situation Room. This president insisted.

"Good morning, Mr. President. With your permission I will begin." General Fitzpatrick remains standing.

"Thomas, aren't you forgetting something?" President John Paul asks without looking at him.

"Sir? ... Oh... yes." he turns to the man next to President John Paul, "Reverend Gibson, will you do the honors of opening our meeting with a prayer?"

"Of course General." With a smug look, the man stands as Major General Fitzpatrick sits. Clasping his hands in front of him, Reverend Gibson leans his head back and clinches his eyes shut. To a man, the others in the room bow their heads, but most simply stare at the table or the floor at their feet. "Almighty Father, Whose Command is over all and Whose Love never fails, let the men in this room be aware of Thy presence and Obedient to Thy will. Keep them true, oh Lord, guarding against dishonesty in purpose and deed while helping our President sweep aside your enemies. Help them remain faithful to the duties this great country has entrusted to them. Let the uniform they wear remind them of the traditions of the Service of which they are but a part. Where there's doubt, steady their faith; where there's temptation, make them strong to resist; where there's fear, bestow upon them courage to continue the fight. We trust in you Jesus, to protect those who love you. Guide these men, oh Lord, with the light of Thy truth, and keep before them the life of Him in whose example and deliverance I trust. Heavenly Father, bless the men who serve our great cause and give the people in this room the strength to carry out your will. In the name of my Lord Jesus Christ, Amen."

"Amen," the room mumbles. The president pats the reverend on the arm as he sits, "Well said Matthew." Turning to General Fitzpatrick, "You may begin now, Thomas." As a rule, the president makes a point of using a person's first name.

"Yes, Mr. President." General Fitzpatrick motions for his aid, Colonel Sanchez, to proceed.

With an aura of professionalism, the colonel moves to stand next to the enormous flat panel screen facing the president. The screen is a relic of a bygone age. He should be giving this presentation using Virtual Reality. However, that's not how President John Paul wants it. The President insists on conducting the Lord's work with the tools He provided. Thus, no one's wearing Earthnet portals and Colonel Sanchez must use old technology.

"At approximately four hundred hours this morning local time, the Islamic Brotherhood attacked the Republic of Luna. The Brotherhoods space fleet is jamming communications but Earth based telescopes recorded a nuclear event that destroyed Lagrange One Space Station and at least one nuclear detonation within Shennong. We don't yet have the full damage assessment..."

While he's talking, the screen behind him shows a series of vids taken from Earth based telescopes. The most telling image is the one showing flame boiling out of Shennong and the subsequent collapse of the mountain.

"What exactly do our sources tell us Walter?" President John Paul asks. The President frequently interrupts briefings. It's something the men have learned to expect. The smart ones, those that have repeatedly been through this meat grinder, design their presentations anticipating and influencing his inevitable intrusions to suit their need.

"Sir, all communications are down. The Brotherhood is jamming all signals. Even laser line-of-sight is overwhelmed because of the intensity of the interference." Colonel Sanchez replies.

"Can we punch through?" the President asks.

"No sir. What we are prepared to do is send in a reconnaissance team," Colonel Sanchez replies.

President John Paul frowns, "In this age of instant communications, all we can do is send someone to have a look?"

"Sir, we are having the same difficulty in communicating with the fleet. The jamming is blanketing every frequency. We cannot risk taking action on disjointed and incomplete information." General Fitzpatrick's gravelly voice grates on the president. "That leaves us with only one alternative, send someone in."

The President's earlier friendliness vanishes, "Thomas, I don't care how it's done but I want to know what's going on and I want to know right now."

"I will dispatch a ship immediately," the General replies.

"What will happen if the Brotherhood catches them during the mission?" Reverend Gibson asks.

Although the reverend holds no office, it doesn't stop him from asking questions. The friendship between the Preacher and the President go back to their college days and the President trusts this self-proclaimed man-of-god explicitly. How else could anyone with a degree in theology obtain a top-level security clearance and the ear of the leader of the most powerful nation on Earth? President John Paul often refers to Reverend Gibson as the Secretary of Religion but there's little doubt that he speaks his mind on a wide variety of issues. No one dares question the arrangement. Self-preservation is a powerful motivator.

"Admiral Greer, will you please respond to the Reverends question?" General Fitzpatrick orders.

"Certainly… Sir, the most likely scenario is that they would all be immediately executed but there's a chance that the Brotherhood would use them as leverage in the arena of world opinion. Worst case is that the Brotherhood would declare war on us. It's better if our men don't get caught," Admiral Greer said.

"That's my prayer as well Admiral." The preacher turns to the president, "but I fail to see what good can come of sending them, John… Even if you learn everything about the situation, what would you do?" The question hangs in the air for a moment. "Are you prepared to go to war to protect godless Lunarians?"

"Let us pray that war is not necessary." Turning back to his Chief of Staff, President John Paul asks, "Thomas, if this escalates beyond the borders of the Republic, are you ready to defend our country and our interests?"

"Sir, we are prepared for any contingency. At the moment our forces are on Alert Level Red," General Fitzpatrick said.

"But if you're not in contact with our space fleet, how do you know what level they are at?" the Preacher asks.

"I know my men. They go by the book and the book explicitly lays out their response. Aggression by any country towards another country will result in our forces going to Alert Level Red. If they or any part of the Federation is attacked, then the Alert Level goes to War Status," General Fitzpatrick explains.

"Well then, I fail to see the need to do any more than what you have already done. I advise letting the infidels handle their own mess. They have had ample time to repent and accept Jesus but have turned their back on Him. Who are we to interfere in His judgment?" Reverend Gibson asks in his best Sunday voice, looking down his long nose at the general.

Feeling his gut twist in revulsion, General Fitzpatrick turns away from the Preacher, "Mr. President, with all due respect for the opinion of Reverend Gibson, we are under treaty obligation to come to the aid of the Republic if and when they are attacked. Do we simply ignore that?" General Fitzpatrick asks.

President John Paul shakes his head and looks thoughtfully at the old general. "Thomas, I agree with Reverend Gibson on this. The Lord is punishing a godless society for their sins and who are we to go against His will? No, I think it's best if I speak with Prince Al Zarqowi and let him know that we will not interfere, just to prevent an accidental escalation of this unfortunate event."

General Fitzpatrick is shocked as are many around the massive table. "Mr. President, I strongly advise against that. Our intelligence indicates the very real possibility that this move is only the start of something much larger."

"Is this that same old idea that the Brotherhood is out to get us?" Reverend Gibson laughs, "As God is my witness, I can assure you, that's not the case. Why is it that every time something happens, you bring up this ridiculous charge? The fanatics who operate at the edges of Islam do not speak for the Caliph and the Islamic Brotherhood. Besides, you of all people should know that the Federation has the most powerful military on the planet. The Brotherhood would be foolish to challenge that. Tell me, am I right? Or is there something you're not sharing with us?"

"Reverend." General Fitzpatrick replies sharply. "History is full of powerful armies being taken by weaker ones. Why are you willing to gamble that the Brotherhood is not planning to attack us?" General Fitzpatrick asks pointedly. Dislike of the Preacher is finally showing through his professionalism.

"I don't gamble. Besides, I thought my source was obvious. It's my

Lord Jesus Christ, praise be His name. *He* will keep us safe from harm because we are a Christian nation under God. *He* will not turn His back on His people." The Preacher said in his best Sunday sermon voice.

"Amen." President John Paul smiles at his friend and turns back to General Fitzpatrick. "Is there anything else this morning Thomas?"

"Sir, isn't it true that the Lord helps those who help themselves?" General Fitzpatrick asks, desperately seeking to make this man see beyond this madness. "I want to go on record as saying it's a mistake not to send a recon team to Luna. We can make sound decisions only if we know what's happening."

The Preacher's face clouds over. "General. Beyond your implication that this is an unsound decision, let me quote from second Chronicles 19:2. *Should thou help the ungodly, and love them that hate the Lord? Therefore is wrath upon thee from the Lord.* Are you suggesting we go against the word of God?"

For a long moment, the old soldier and the Preacher lock horns, neither willing to back down. "We've given our word. Does that mean anything?" the General growls.

"At ease Thomas. I've made my decision and now it's your duty to see that it's carried out." President John Paul pushes back from the table and rises. The other men in the room scramble to their feet.

"Yes sir. Thank you sir." General Fitzpatrick said. The president and his entourage leave the room as fast as they arrived.

The preacher leans down and said something in President John Paul's ear who nods agreement. It's time to retire Thomas Fitzpatrick. However, the president puts a stop to any talk of reeducation. He forgives his friend's vindictiveness, dismissing it as the exception that shows him to be human.

Back in the Situation Room, "That went well, don't you think?" Admiral Greer said dryly to his boss. The two go back many years and speak bluntly to one another.

"Sir?" Colonel Sanchez said, "I didn't complete my presentation. The president doesn't know about the troop movements or their space fleet."

"When's the last time that anybody managed to complete a presidential presentation?" The old general shakes his head, "Nothing could have changed his mind. He walked in here knowing he was going to let the Lunarians fight the Brotherhood alone. Now he's going to go tell the Prince that the Federation will not interfere. I fear the message the Caliph will hear is one of weakness. Let's do what we can to ready ourselves for war, gentlemen."

Art of War

Cris stops the cycle next to the smashed vehicle. It's one of the rovers sent to track him down after Hallstead. He needs what's inside its fuel tanks. He rummages around in the cycle's small tool compartment until he finds the universal interconnect. Only then does he realize he's not alone.

At least two dozen heavily armed bugeyes are confronting him. Cris whispers a goodbye into his visor, expecting to die in the next instant. If the device survived, at least his family would know he was thinking of them in his final moments.

Instead of opening fire, one of them transmits in broken English. "Remove your weapons."

When Cris remains motionless, the voice repeats, "You will remove your weapons or die."

They wish to capture him? *Interesting.* Cris shows them his hands then slowly removes and drops his pistol. As he draws the sword from over his shoulder, an excited shuffle runs through the soldiers like wind across a wheat field.

They waste no time binding Cris hand and foot, shoving a thick black hood over his head and stuffing him into a rover's empty tool locker. He barely fits. The bone-jarring ride takes the better part of three hours, only the last fifteen minutes on a smooth roadway.

The soldiers pull Cris from the box, letting him fall to the ground. They do not expect him able to stand after his brutal ride but the Highlander surprises them. He gracefully gets to his feet with no apparent ill effects from the rough handling. Someone barks an order. Two soldiers, one on each arm, grab Cris and hustle him forward. It ends when the soldiers force him to his knees and jerk the hood off. Going from utter blackness to glaring light should have disorientated him, but his visor easily adjusts to the sudden change, all the while recording everything for posterity.

The Highlander is at the center of attention. Intense floodlights bear down on him from the tops of troop carriers. The carriers form a high wall along one side of the road as far as he can see. A steep mountainside defines the other.

Cris is in the midst of the Army of Islam. All around him is a sea of bugeyes. Hundreds of Brotherhood soldiers have gathered on the road, on the tops of the nearby carriers, and well up the mountain creating a makeshift arena. Looking beyond them, Cris identifies this place as one of the double-wide segments of Kahfah Road, deciding which one takes only a few moments longer.

Alone, kneeling in the dust of Luna, surrounded by enemies, Cris calmly looks around. The crowd parts and a tall figure in black armor walks through. Rising to his feet, Cris turns to face him. This man's vacsuit is different, the fish scale is finer with barely a reflection, and the helmet smaller and less bug-like.

"Bring me his sword," the man said in Arabic, motioning impatiently. Usually, a subject cringes when going from complete blackness to intense light, but it doesn't seem to bother this infidel at all. Instead, a shiver runs down his spine at the inhuman coolness exhibited by the Lunarian. What can one expect from Djinn? It's further confirmation that these creatures are evil.

41

One of the soldiers delivers the sword to the bugeye.

"Where did you get this?" The tall man asked in English.

"Made it," Cris answers.

"Unusually thin and much too fragile for a true sword," he scowls. "This could not possibly be used in a fight."

"There's only one way to find out," Cris said.

The officer moves to confront Cris, throwing the Lunarian's sword at his feet. In a single fluid motion, the officer pulls his own broad curved blade from its scabbard and cuts the vacuum centimeters from the Highlander's face. Cris never flinches.

"**This** is a sword, infidel." Pointing at the smaller blade lying in the dust with the tip of his sword, he said, "That is a toy." Speaking to someone behind Cris, the man orders in Arabic, *"Untie him."*

Addressing the crowd, the man raises the sword above his head and continues, *"You shall all see the will of Allah. This Djinn shall die by my sword."*

Turning back to Cris, he commands in English, "Pick it up."

Cris obliges and retrieves his sword. The two men are roughly the same height but the officer is heavier and wearing an armored vacsuit. The Highlander is in the black and gray camouflage of the Lunarian Police Department. While both vacsuits incorporate sophisticated puncture resistant materials, a determined blade will breach them. The crowd presses forward with excitement.

The officer attacks first, swinging his heavy sword in a mighty blow. Cris parries and sidesteps with speed and grace.

The Lunarian blade is lighter than the scimitar and Cris skilled in its use, but one wrong move and his sword will shatter as though made of glass. Back and forth, the two men fight, each measuring the other, probing for weakness. As the seconds turn to minutes, the Brotherhood officer has a growing realization that for all the many hours of practice that lies behind him, he's not the master in this duel. He's never faced a blade so fast and now is fighting a defensive battle. It's all he can do just to stay alive.

Cris presses, never giving his opponent a chance to regroup, hitting the man's armor at will. Each blow is but a note in the silent symphony that is this duel to the death.

Growing evermore desperate, the officer grabs one of his soldiers and shoves him at Cris, boring in behind to make the kill.

Cris is too fast, playing off the surprised soldier to mask his own final assault. The officer never sees the one that gets him.

Faster than a striking viper, the thin Lunarian blade slides upward, forcing its way between the layers of armor, rending heart and lung asunder, then out again as quickly as it went in. The Highlander takes joy in the sound it sends up his arm. He cannot see the face behind the bugeye but in that moment, Cris knows the weight of hate's full measure.

The Highlander thrusts his sword Earthward, blood boiling from its length in a gaseous haze.

Maximizing his visors transmission signal, Cris bellows in perfect Arabic, *"Behold, the will of Allah."*

The soldiers are stunned. Most stand frozen, unable to reconcile what they are witnessing. Only a few take action and bring their weapons to bear but they are far too late.

Agile as a big cat and much quicker, Cris runs and leaps effortlessly over the nearest transport. Those gathered on its top scatter like a brood of chicks under the shadow of a hawk. The Highlander disappears into the darkness beyond before anyone can fire a shot.

ЯL

Tempel set a flight plan that took them due north out of Scottsbluff almost to Albategnius Crater then northwest. They approach the Trans Lunar Highway (TLH) a couple kilometers south of Purgatory. Farpoint is to the north.

Sam leads the way with a spybot. Both Moonhawks hang back. Somehow, they must get across the road undetected. It's not a trivial task.

"We must assume the battlestation in Lagrange One is monitoring the road. It's what I'd do. It's in the perfect location to look down on the Republic," Tempel said.

"They can watch the entire road?" Lazarus asks.

"Sure. The compacted roadbed itself is the perfect background to reveal movement. It will silhouette us like a puppet in a shadow play," Tempel said.

"Then how do we get across?" Lazarus asks.

"We find a place where the road is shaded from their line-of-sight. The TLH runs almost due north and south here but there are a few spots where it runs along the base of a south-facing cliff," Sam said.

Sam isn't worried about the spybot running out of fuel on this mission. She has enough to go many kilometers, scouting ahead for the Moonhawks.

"It's over the next rise," Tempel tells Sam. He's less than a hundred meters behind. Just ahead of them is the Siamese Twins, two small craters each about a kilometer in diameter but only a half kilometer apart. Lunarian geologists determined the two craters formed at almost the exact same instant in a twin impact. Complex fluid dynamics resulted in a cliff several hundred meters high along their southern rim. The Trans Lunar Highway passes within a few meters of its base.

The spybot clears the ridge. The TLH is less than a kilometer away. Road construction crews scooped the regolith from a path eighty meters wide and a meter deep, compressing the material into a hard surface forty meters wide and twenty centimeters thick, a ten to one compaction ratio. Sam scans up and down the road. The color of undisturbed lunar regolith in starlight is gray. The highway is a ribbon of lighter compacted material surrounded by the darker color of disturbed regolith.

"That's it," Sam said.

"Why do you sound worried?" Lazarus asks.

"If it's only the battlestation in Lagrange One that's watching, this is perfect. But if there are other ships watching, they may have a better angle to spot us," Sam said.

"And don't forget the bugs. The Brotherhood may have spread bugs all along the road, especially someplace like this," Corazon adds.

"Corazon, sweep for bugs as we go in. Consuela, let's take this route," Tempel sketches his proposed path on a virtual map.

"We can cross here… hug the base of the cliff until we get here…" Tatiana adds.

"Aye, sounds like a plan. Tempel, I'm on your six," Consuela said.

The spybot led the Moonhawks down the slope. Tempel eases forward never getting higher than ten meters and or faster than thirty kph.

The closer they come to the Trans Lunar Highway, the higher the risk of detection. All they had to do was look up at max zoom to see the hulking form of the battlestation hanging over their heads. They want to cross fast and disappear back into the highlands.

On the way in, they detect nothing. No bugs. No patrols. *Nothing?* Even the roadbed itself looks normal. Tempel records the crossing with his sensors on maximum. It didn't appear that an army had come this way. *Strange.*

They leave the highway behind and head for Aldrin Station, keeping their distance from several bombed out structures along the way. They stay off the roads and finally land a few kilometers from the base of Rim Mountain.

Sam flies the spybot to a landing on a high ridge. Using its main sensor array, Tempel zooms in on activity about a kilometer away. "That's Franklin Gate." The place is swarming with Brotherhood.

Goliaths bristling with cannons lurk within spitting distance of the huge airlock door. Soldiers have set up a checkpoint right outside the gate using two troop carriers.

"We're definitely not going through there," Lazarus said.

Tempel zooms out, points the camera about half way up Rim Mountain and searches for a moment. Finding something, he zooms in revealing a small bullseye carved in the stone. Aiming the spybots communications laser at the symbol, Tempel said, "Aldrin Station, do you copy?"

Magi acknowledges the relay nanoseconds later. "Greetings Tempel. It's good to see you."

Tempel sighs. A couple gigawatts of tension evaporate at the sight of her face. "Greetings, Magi. It's good to be seen."

"Tempel." Corso rumbles. He's the first of thousands to link realtime over the next few seconds. This is big news. Everyone is tuning in. "Where are you?"

"Outside Franklin Gate," Tempel replies. "We have four casualties including Captain Osaka."

Corso sighs, "I'm sorry to hear that. He was a good man and he taught you well lieutenant. You have brought Quan Kiai home."

"We're not home yet. Franklin Gate is crawling with Brotherhood," Tempel said.

"Go to Miller's Farm. It's about two klicks south of Franklin."

"Aye, I know where it is," Tempel replies.

The area around Randsburg is some of the worst badlands in the region. Sheer cliffs and deep ravines are the norm. Most travelers stay on the road if they have any sense.

Cris didn't care. The Highlander makes his own path, freely scampering up and down the steep mountainsides.

The road is especially difficult the last few kilometers leading into Randsburg. In many places, it's barely wide enough for a single Goliath. It goes up and down like a yoyo, clinging precariously onto the steep mountainsides. Passing lanes are few and far between and most of them are at the bottom of deep canyons.

Cris is crossing a ridge near one of these pulloffs when he notices something odd alongside the road far below. They're crosses. He can see seven, about twenty meters apart, standing upright facing the road. He slows and magnifies. There's something on the cross members. A low growl rises unbidden from deep in his chest. He turns and moves straight down the steep slope towards the crosses.

The Highlander can't believe what he's seeing. The passing lane is about a kilometer long. Along it, he counts thirty-nine crosses and forty dead people. They had stripped the bodies, skewered them on a cross and left them to the vacuum. What evil could possess a human being to do such a thing?

The shriveled up victims look like they're sitting on the cross members. The vertical poles enter their rectum and emerge near their clavicle forcing their heads to tilt to the side at an odd angle.

Impaled upon one cross is a second tiny body. Cris assumes it was a baby. He can't tell if the other dehydrated corpse was male or female.

Cris stands on the road looking up. Empty eye sockets stare back, their leathery faces drawn tight to their skulls. Cris could never have imagined anything so horrible. Rage builds inside him.

These were citizens. Not soldiers. Not warmongers. Law-abiding Lunarian citizens. And these ghastly crosses... The Brotherhood must have brought them here for this very purpose. The fitting on the bottom next to the ground is for a Construction Utility Vehicle used to drive the crosses into the regolith. A sick mind thought this up, and a sicker heart did the deed.

If the Brotherhood meant to scare him, they failed miserably. It had the exact opposite effect. Cris snarls and turns to face the rovers racing towards him. He leaps off the road and runs down a side canyon, his black and gray uniform affording him near perfect camouflage. The rovers follow firing as they come but Cris is virtually invisible once he's off the roadway.

Cris could easily leave the vehicles behind. They are limited to the relative flatness at the bottom. All he need do was climb up and over the side of the canyon and he would disappear into the rugged landscape beyond. Instead, he draws them in.

The four rovers bounce down the narrow canyon, their lasers firing as fast as they recharge, but the shots are wild, without any real target. The canyon narrows even further and becomes impassable a short way ahead. Cris turns and heads up the steep mountainside and over the ridge then doubles back.

He waits until the rovers have passed then leaps upon the roll cage of the last one, draws his sword, and plunges it into the driver. The rover veers into the side of the canyon. The impact throws Cris headlong towards the rock face. Agile as a cat, he twists in midair and lands on his feet and hands.

Leaping back on the rover, he slaps the safety harness free and drags the stunned passenger from the vehicle. Holding him up with his left hand, Cris impales the man with his sword. He quickly strips the body of its pistol and holster before throwing the corpse aside.

Laser light spatters against the nearby rock face. The other three rovers are returning. Cris races back down the canyon away from them but never getting too far ahead. He picks a rather sharp bend to make his next move.

Again, he climbs the steep mountainside and circles back. He draws his newly acquired pistol and targets the lead rover, shredding its fuel tanks. A moment later, the hypergolic fuels mix and explode in silent fury. Its carcass blocks the canyon. The other two rovers will need to move it before they can leave.

The four remaining soldiers are frantic. They don't know where the Highlander is. The shots could have come from anywhere. The silent lunar mountains loom over them. They are alone on a strange world fighting against an unholy monster. They panic. The lead rover rams the mangled remains of its brethren desperately trying to force its way past. The two rovers get tangled and grind to a stop.

The passenger jumps out and begins franticly pushing the dead rover out of the way. Together, man and machine move the wreckage aside. The soldier waves at the other rover before getting back in. They are strangely silent.

Something's wrong. He looks closer. A blood red fog is gathering around the two soldiers. He throws himself into his rover screaming at his partner, *"Go."* but they remain where they are. *"Go. Go. Go."* he screams repeatedly. When he looks at his comrade, he realizes the man is sitting behind the wheel, dead. The red haze of death rises slowly from the corpse.

"Noooooo." A blade flashes in the starlight and the screaming stops.

Cris wipes his sword clean and continues towards Randsburg. A tiny spybot follows.

ЯL

The surface portion of Miller's Farm had been a collection of half-buried large-diameter prefab metal cylinders sealed end-to-end and laid out side-to-side like rows in a field. During the fourteen days of daylight, louvers built above them would reflect natural sunlight through Duraglass windows. During darkness, the louvers would reposition and reflect the interior sunlamps onto the plants inside. Each row had contained many acres of high-density hydroponics. The bombardment hadn't spared them. They lay in ruins.

Old man Miller had tucked his farmhouse deep under Rim Mountain where it was not only protected from meteorites, it could share processing and recycling facilities with Aldrin Station. The attack had mangled the outer airlock but left the access tunnel leading to the farm unharmed. Looking down from the battlestation hanging above them, the airlock would look impassible but Tempel had no problem flying his Moonhawk past it. He flew down the tunnel and landed in the farm's main hanger. A moment later, Consuela landed her ship beside his.

Corso is waiting when they lowered the ramps and walked off the Moonhawks. Behind Corso is a vidcasting crowd of Quan Kiai's family and friends. Tens of thousands more are linked to watch. Corso motions for them to form up. Tempel takes his usual place as Senior Lieutenant.

Tatiana looks at Tempel and shakes her head, "Tempel, what are you doing? Take the front." She pushes him in the general direction.

"I can't take Kitajima's place," Tempel resists.

"No one's asking you to. Just stand up front," Tatiana replies.

"Aye," "go for it," "it's only right," Quan Kiai picks their new leader in those few seconds. Tempel accepts and moves to face his platoon. Tatiana takes his place as Senior Lieutenant.

Tatiana's voice breaks but she maintains her discipline. "Captain Kitajima Osaka, KIA. Special Teams Officer Brice Guyart, KIA. Special Teams Officer Lei Cheung, KIA. Special Teams Officer Karl Svensson, KIA. All present or accounted for lieutenant,"

"Thank you lieutenant. Quan Kiai, form up in four-man teams. Let's bring our comrades home," Tempel orders. "Sam, Kipper, you're with me. Master Sergeant Hackling… let's go get Kitajima."

"Aye," she manages to say. Hack will do her crying later.

Four at a time, they climb the ramp and carry a black body bag back down. They reverently place them on the ER vehicle.

After the last bag had been loaded and Quan Kiai reformed, Tempel

50

does a sharp about-face. "Quan Kiai present or accounted for," he calls out.

Corso had watched the entire event unfold without saying a word. He now moves forward until he was before Tempel and salutes, "Welcome home. Thank you all for a job well done. I wish I could tell you that's it's over but I can't. There's a General Council in session right now and you're all invited, including you, Lazarus."

A personal invitation by Aldrin Station's Security Chief is not something he can refuse. "Aye," Lazarus said. It's the first time he's used the Lunarian slang.

"Corso. Let them take a shower and unwind. They have been through a lot." Liz is one of the few people in Aldrin Station who dare to speak to Corso this way.

Corso chuckles, "Aye, you're right, and when you're right, your right. Join us in Council when you're ready. Just don't take too long."

"Aye," Tempel nods.

Randsburg

Randsburg is Luna's only gold mine. It also produces platinum, palladium, iridium, osmium, rhenium, rhodium, ruthenium and a lot of iron. The prevailing theory is the giant iron meteor that formed Arzachel Crater was extremely rich in iron-loving or siderophile elements. The impact scattered the rare metals and iron into the craters rim in lumps, like raisins in oatmeal.

John Rand and his partner Bill Langdon discovered the deposit in 2076. Keenly aware of the importance of properly recording their claim before a rush could get started, John devised a clever scheme that bought them some time. Fearful that other miners from Hallstead and Prattville would soon be over to investigate, the two prospectors loaded up their rover with bags of low-grade chromite and headed for Prattville.

Curious miners asked what they had found. John stubbornly held out but finally admitted, "Well... I think we've found something pretty good." He would say no more. The inquisitive miners soon found the planted bags while John and Bill were away. Word spread throughout camp about the two fools digging chromite in the middle of the badlands. It gave the partners an extra day or two to stake their claims. They called their discovery the Goosefoot Mine.

Randsburg is a typical mining town. Starting from a single Quonset, it has evolved into a thriving subterranean city of over eleven thousand. It doesn't have the enormous malls or commonways like Aldrin Station. Instead, Randsburg grew out of the excavations that harvested the ore. Thus, it's a mishmash of irregular tunnels and strangely shaped rooms spread out over a very large volume.

Approaching the town's main entrance, Cris moves along the ridge overlooking the road. The road ends in a box canyon surrounded by high, steep mountains. Thousands of tons of iron pass through this gate on its way to the smelters in Prattville and Aldrin Station.

The open area outside Ransburg's main gate is not very large, about a hundred meters square. The initial bombardment reached even here. Nothing remains standing but the wreckage has been shoved aside making room for a Brotherhood force of at least two thousand soldiers. Several heavily armed Goliaths stand guard at the massive airlock door, which is wide open. More Goliaths protect the few road construction vehicles they have left. Guards watch from the tops of the troop carriers and rovers run patrols up and down the line. They have learned.

The rock beneath him heaves and explodes throwing Cris off the summit. He tumbles down the steep mountainside. More shots follow. They're coming from above. The Brotherhood's gunships have spotted him and are maneuvering to get a better angle.

Dazed but unhurt, Cris regains control and turns his downward momentum into forward motion. He races across the vertical landscape but he can't lose the fighters. They follow him. He must have picked up a bot coming in.

Cris retreats to the darkest shadows at the bottom of a deep canyon. The fighters can't follow him down here but they can still shoot. They narrowly miss repeatedly. He probes for the spybot while he runs.

If I were a bot, where would I hide? Cris doubles back and scrambles up the side of the rill looking for the faint thermal signature. There, on the ledge, the bot's tiny thrusters had heated the stone when it landed moments before. Cris draws and fires in one smooth motion. The tiny sliver of rock disintegrates. He doesn't stick around to see if it was the right rock. That will soon become apparent.

He races down the canyon leaving the fighters behind to shoot at shadows. Searchlights and lasers probe the darkness but Cris is already a kilometer away and moving fast. It was the right rock.

Cris cuts across deep canyons and sharp ridges making his way to the top of Arzachel Crater's rim mountain. He cautiously approaches Randsburg's main spaceport. It is one of the highest and busiest ports in the Republic. Most of the precious metals pass through here. The bombardment had pounded it into rubble. Small craters pockmark the flattened mountaintop and unrecognizable twisted metal is all that remains of its ships and installations.

Beyond the spaceport looms the massive solar refinery. It looks intact. The Brotherhood must have plans for it. He scrambles down the inside of rim and comes to a small observation balcony overlooking the vast Arzachel Crater. Cris looks around carefully before dropping upon it like a cougar coming home.

The airlock door is closed. He places his left hand on its pad. When it doesn't immediately open, he backs off finding a spot a few meters away. He settles down to wait.

Minutes go by. Finally, the door opens and swings wide but nothing else happens. Then a girl tentatively steps out looking around the empty balcony. She carries a disrupter and is ready to use it. "Cris?" She turns to go back inside when Cris drops down beside her.

The girl jumps, "Cris. Don't scare me like that." Her pistol slides back into its holster.

"I need to speak with John." Cris moves past the girl.

"You don't have time for a simple greeting?" She pulled the door shut and locked it. The airlock cycled quickly.

"Greetings Callista," Cris said opening the inner door.

"Greetings Cristobal. John's at the refinery. He told me to get some food in you." Callista runs but can't keep up. "Cris, slow down."

The Highlander pauses and looks back irritably.

Callista studies Cris as she catches up. "Cris... what's wrong?"

"There's an army outside your door and you ask me what's wrong?"

"Yes, I know. We've been able to block them but only because they can't bring those damned Goliath's into the city."

They're moving fast but at a human pace. Cris has been inside Randsburg many times. He knows where he's going almost as well as Callie.

"Magi?" Cris calls.

"Magi's gone. The attack cut us off without a single thread," Callie said. Cris is acting strange. They are good friends but she doesn't know this person. This man is cold and angry.

"Are you hungry?"

"After I talk to John," Cris didn't bite her head off but it was close.

"Fine..." Callie slows and lets the Highlander go on alone. "Nice seeing you Cris..."

Cris ignores her and speeds up again. He enters the refinery from one of the upper entrances and descends to the main floor using his hands and feet. He spots John about the same instant that John spots him.

"Greetings Cris. It's good to see you." John walks toward the Highlander. "Do you bring word from Aldrin Station?"

"Greetings... No... I was hoping you knew something. I was on patrol when this started."

"Bill's getting a Moonhawk ready. He's going to make a run to Prattville. Can you tell us anything about what's between us and them?" John asks.

"I can do more than that. We need to summarize and authenticate my visor records and add them to his manifest." Cris said.

Callie walks up behind him, "I can help with that."

Cris glances at her and said to John, "We should get someone… older…"

"I'm seventeen. I vote, I work, I fight." Callie flares. "What more do you want?"

John can tell by Cris's expression that something was out of the ordinary here, "She's a grown woman. She can handle it."

Cris turns to Callie.

"Don't look so sad," Callie said. "How bad can it be?"

"Callie…" He fears shredding what's left of her childhood and the thought makes him feel like shit.

She puts her hand on his arm, "Cris, I can do this."

Cris lowers his eyes and turns away. There's only one way to make her understand. "Very well…" He downloads the vid of his last few days to her visor. She divides the work and begins.

"You could use a shower and some real food," John said.

"Aye, and some sleep," Cris said wearily. "But first, tell me what's happening?"

John sighs, "The attack came just after sunset. We lost all satellite communications and Magi abandoned us without a single thread remaining in town. Then the bombs came. They killed fourteen outside the main gate, forty in the spaceport and many more out on the crater floor. Then the soldiers show up and start shooting. We got everyone out that we could and made a stand here at the refinery. So far, they haven't been able to get past Conrad and his warriors."

"Conrad's here?" Cris is relieved.

"Aye, we would be in bad shape if they weren't."

"I will report to him immediately." Cris starts to stand.

"Hold on," John reaches out and grips Cris by the arm. "He's doing fine. He already knows you're here and will talk to you after you're properly fed and rested."

"Fine," Cris is too tired to argue. He sits and eats in stoic silence not tasting any of it.

With tears streaming down her cheeks, Callie comes and sits down next to him. She lays her head on his shoulder and puts her arm about his waist. "It's so horrible, what they did to our people on those crosses. Oh Cris. I'm so sorry…" She thinks about the number of people he killed. No wonder he's different.

As others view the summary and realize what Cris has done, they gather around the Highlander. John Rand walks over and sits across from Cris. He watches the young Lunarian eat for a few minutes before saying. "You will forever have my support and appreciation for what you've been through," John said.

"Many are dead because of me," Cris pushes the half-empty plate away.

"Aye, but many Lunarians are alive because of you. Don't forget that. You fought back and for that, we're all grateful."

"I'm a Highlander. It's what we do." Cris is suddenly very tired.

John reaches across the table and grips the young man's arm. "Aye, and we all appreciate it." John looks at Callie, "Take Cris to my billet and get him showered. Find him a bunk. I'll see to it that you're not disturbed."

"Aye," a shower and some sleep sounds good to Cris…

ℜ𝕃

Quan Kiai is loud and boisterous entering the crew quarters in Dakota Warren. The warrior's help each other peel away the artificial epidermis that has kept them alive and well on their airless world. The suits go straight away into the vacsuit rehab modules and the Highlanders head for the shower.

Lindsey helps Lazarus remove his vacsuit and he helps her. Lazarus does his best not to stare at those around him. They're the last to leave.

57

"You've had a chance to view some of your father's records. What are your thoughts?" Lindsey asks. They're in the ramp leading to the shower.

"He was running away from my mother," Lazarus said frankly. "Apparently, she didn't know anything about my tool shed education because if she had, she would have turned us in. At least that's what he thought." He glances at her swaying tits and stumbles.

Lindsey grins and grips his arm tightly. "What do you think? Would she turn you in?" She asked.

Lazarus thinks for a moment, "She may have turned in my little brother. You have to know my mom. She's intensely religious."

They enter the bath and pass between the polished stone columns into the communal shower beyond. Scattered about singly, the Lunarians are strangely motionless under the running water.

"What're they doing?" Lazarus asks. Warm water envelopes him but cannot distract him from staring at the warriors.

"They're viewing summaries of the events that have transpired since we've been gone." Lindsey replies.

"Summaries?"

"Magi strings together pertinent moments into summaries like she did with your father's vids. She can compress a day into a few minutes," Lindsey said. "See for yourself, link with Tempel."

He does. Sights, sounds, and smells assail Lazarus. He staggers and might have fallen if Lindsey hadn't been there.

"Easy does it," she said putting her arm around him.

Lazarus concentrates and begins to discern events at speeds much faster than normal. He's in a commonway fighting… at a table eating… working on a machine… talking… crying… The words are a high-pitched screech, the images a blur.

"How fast is it going?" Lazarus asks.

"Everyone is different. Tempel is one of the fastest at about sixty-six times normal," Lindsey said.

"Sixty-six. He understands what he's seeing?"

"Aye. In fact, his recall is better after high speed viewing than after normal," she adds.

As if on cue, Quan Kiai finishes the summaries and gathers in a circle, facing inward with their arms around each other. Lindsey pulls Lazarus into the mix.

Lazarus is uneasy but Lindsey holds him firmly on one side with Sam on the other. He tries to be nonchalant but everywhere he looks is wet glistening flesh. He's the meat between Sam's warm body on one side and Lindsey's on the other.

Lindsey senses his nervousness, "Relax." She hopes he wasn't going to be a problem.

"I'm trying." he said sneaking a peek at the nudity all around him. Knowing where to look, he can now see the subtle changes in their bodies while admiring the grace and elegance of the Highlanders. They are beautiful and he finds himself staring.

Consuela looks over at Lazarus. "So this is what an Earthman looks like? Kind of soft if you ask me, except that rod between your legs."

"I must admit, I am not accustomed to seeing so many beautiful ladies in the flesh. My mind and body seem to have different ideas about how to handle it. I do apologize," Lazarus said.

The Highlanders roar with laughter, perhaps more than is warranted. Consuela smiles, "Well said Earthman. But you really must do something about that body. Put on a little muscle."

"I like him just the way he is," Lindsey chimes in, squeezing his butt cheek for emphasis.

Consuela shrugs, "No accounting for taste."

The group closes the circle ever tighter. They make a solid mass of human flesh huddled in the center of the shower. Streams of hot water create a fog that engulfs them in its warm embrace.

"Karl Svensson, Lei Cheung, Brice Guyart, Kitajima Osaka." Tempel said each name slowly and deliberately.

"Nell Goddard," Sam adds.

Tempel glances at her and nods. "We celebrate their lives and honor our fallen comrades with our deeds and actions."

"**We shall remember.**" Lindsey and the warriors join voices and speak as one, their naked bodies shimmering wetly under the hot water.

Only Lazarus remains mute. From the outside looking in, this gathering has all the earmarks of a nudist prayer meeting but without any mention of god or life after death. Humanity is a social animal and these young men and women are saying goodbye to their friends. In a philosophy that does not pretend to an afterlife, death is not a transition, rather an ending.

"They purchased our freedom with their lives," Tempel said.

"**We shall never forget,**" Quan Kiai said in unison. Their tears are lost in the shower's steady downpour but the raw emotion is palpable. They will miss their friends.

"There is no greater love than that which they have shown. They have sacrificed their existence so that we may live." Tempel shuts his eyes and envisions Brice, Karl, Lei and Kitajima. He has known them his entire life and they him. Now, in the safety of his home, it didn't seem real that they were dead.

"**We shall honor them always.**"

"We, the survivors, accept their sacrifice and pledge to bring it honor," Tempel said fiercely.

"**Study the past, live in the present, and plan for the future.**" Quan Kiai said.

Tempel looks around at his friends, one arm around Sam's waist, hers about his. His other arm holds Zoey tightly. His heart aches for those missing and he can sense the pain in those around him. Nothing will bring the dead back to life but they do have the public records. As

60

one, they begin to chant…

Lo, there do I see my Mother and my Father…

Lo, there do I see my Sisters and my Brothers…

Lo, there do I see my Ancestors back to the Beginning…

They beckon me to Take my place among Them…

In the Hallowed Halls of Remembrance…

Where we All live on Forever…

Brice appears in the center of the circle, smirking like always, "Quick. What's the difference between heaven and hell? … Give up? … Nothing. They're both figments of wishful thinking," he laughs. His image remains untouched by the shower's water.

Quan Kiai collectively groans. Leave it to Brice to record a death message like this. They can't help but grin.

"If you're viewing this then I must be dead. What the fuck, over. I probably screwed up but whatever happened, don't worry about it. I'm not… I'm dead. Remember?" Brice said with overzealous sincerity. Then he tucks the smile away and turns serious, "I have recorded something for each of you but the main thing for everyone to do right now is just carry on. Never give up. Never quit. Finish the job…" He shifts his gaze around the circle as if looking at each friend. Lazarus shivers as it passes over him. Then as suddenly as it disappeared, the smirk returns, "Bye bye… Adios… So long… Farewell… Arrividerci… Auf Wiedersehen…" his voice and image fades away.

One by one, Karl, Lei and Kitajima take his place. They each have recorded a brief death message for the platoon.

Kitajima is last. "Attention." he barks out and they all snap straight, even Lazarus. "At ease. Y 'all are probably in the shower, seems like you spend a god-awful amount of time in there… No sad faces. I won't stand for that. Don't waste your time grieving over me. I had a long life and a good one thanks to you people and the Republic. Working with all of you gave me something I sorely needed, respect from people I respect... No matter how I ended up dead, I want you all to know that I have absolutely no regrets. I would do it all over again in a New York minute."

Kitajima turns slowly looking out at the platoon, nodding in that way he had of drawing your complete attention to what he was about to say. "Death is only painful for the living," he remains dry amidst the downpour but only Lazarus finds that odd. "Death is a hard thing to wrap your mind around. Oh sure, we all know we are eventually going to die but that's always in the future, not now, not today, but the fact is, it catches up to all of us. There's nothing to do about it. Accept it and move on."

Kitajima snaps to attention, "It's been a pleasure," He thrusts his fist upward, "Quan Kiai..."

The warriors press into an even tighter circle, their fists joining Kitajima's one last time, "**Quan Kiai,**" they respond in unison, just before he fades away.

The circle breaks up. It takes a few seconds for Lazarus to realize that the ceremony is over. Lindsey takes him by the hand and the two of them find a nearby bench, luxuriating in the hot water cascading over their bare skin.

The shower soon fills with laughter and horseplay. Soapsuds and playful scrubbing inevitably turns into a different kind of tension relieving activity. Moans of pleasure and the rhythmic sounds of human passion replace laughter.

Lazarus, completely attentive of Lindsey, finds it absurdly easy to embrace the open sexuality of the Lunarians. It's a natural and nurturing thing. He makes a strange happy sound, half laugh, half sigh. Lindsey looks down at him. He meets her gaze and winks. She smiles.

Free at last. Free at last. Great god almighty, I am free at last.

ЯL

Councilor Taylor asks impatiently. "Can we get down to business?"

"By all means, proceed," Abby said.

"The situation's not critical at the moment. We should take this opportunity to send ambassadors to work out a diplomatic solution to the conflict," Councilor Taylor declares.

"They've nuked Shennong. They've nuked Lagrange One and replaced it with a battlestation. They've invaded our city threatening to nuke us. Their space fleet is jamming the entire system. They have a battlestation hanging over our heads ready to turn Aldrin Station into a crater. Moreover, there is an army coming down Kahfah Road. I would say the situation is extremely critical," Councilor Debouch replies.

"We must at least try," Councilor Taylor said. "Diplomacy has its place."

"Their idea of a peaceful solution is our annihilation. We can't surrender. We must fight. Their space fleet is our number one threat. It can destroy us all. It must be neutralized," Corso said.

Abby nods in agreement, "Corso's right. Whatever we decide to do, dealing with their warships must be at the top of the list. Diplomacy can come later."

"They must be destroyed. There's no other way," Lazarus said.

Only Lindsey pays attention and turns to him. "We aren't strong enough Lazarus. The Treaty of Independence has seen to that." she said. "We have no space fleet of our own."

"The Chinese do," he retorts.

Abby turns her attention to Lazarus and Lindsey.

"They haven't lifted a finger to help us so far. Why should they change now?" Lindsey asks.

"We invite them to come out and play," Lazarus said. A few more citizens have linked and the growing number attracting the attention of the Councilors. With a gesture, Abby draws Lindsey and Lazarus down to the Assembly Floor. Lazarus runs his fingers through his long hair, gazing nervously at the multitude around him. He has given presentations before but never been the focus like this. He likes it. He turns to face Abby.

"That's absurd," Councilor Taylor declares.

Abby ignores him and asks Lazarus. "How do you propose to do that?"

"We use a Brotherhood nuke to attack a Chinese battlestation," Lazarus said.

"All that would accomplish is to have two superpowers at war with us," Councilor Taylor said. "I can assure you young man, that conflict would be a very short one."

"Not if they think the Brotherhood attacked them… That just might work," Abby said. "How would you do it?"

"The Chinese navy will be very nervous right now. The jamming is keeping them from communicating with their ships just like everybody else. They're not going to know as much as we do about the situation. They would have seen what happened to Shennong and Lagrange. They may even think the Republic is defeated. I'll bet my retirement that every vessel in space is on full alert. All we need to do is push them over the edge," Lazarus said.

"The Chinese are allied with the Brotherhood. Why not draw the Federation into the conflict?" Abby asks.

"The Chinese fleet is bigger," Lazarus said.

Abby frowns, sensing something in Lazarus she didn't like, the faint whiff of deceit. She looks closely at his polygraphic indicators. It's obvious. Despite everything, there's still some Federation loyalty within the man.

"That may be true but the Christians have been in conflict with the Muslims for generations while the Chinese have helped the Brotherhood almost from the beginning," Abby replies. "It makes more sense to draw the Federation in."

"You sure you don't have some other reason for leaving the Federation out of it?" Corso growls.

Lazarus is not one to give up so easily. "My family and friends live there… so yes, maybe I do have some other motive for not wanting the Federation at war," Lazarus admits.

Corso and Abby look at each other. Lazarus had almost slipped but was now telling the truth. Corso nods, "I like the basic idea but we need to expand it. We have twelve nukes. I suggest we spread them around. If nothing else it will cause confusion."

"To do it right, you will need detailed information on the location and size of every vessel in orbital space. How will you get that?" Councilor Debouch asks.

A giant 3D graphic of cislunar space appears in the central area of the chamber. Floating letters identifies Taurus Colony, Hyundai Shipyards and many of the satellites that inhabit Earths orbital space.

"After triangulating each jamming signal, one at a time, Magi found sixty-five sources, three battlestations, two heavy cruisers, eighteen destroyers and forty-two frigates," Corso said. Orange dots appear within the graphic, the bigger the dot, the bigger the ship.

"That's the Brotherhood. What about the rest?" Councilor Debouch asks.

"The locations of all other military vessels are extrapolations from data obtained just before the attack. Each hour that passes makes their location less certain. China… Japan… European Union… India… Brazil… Australia…" Corso adds their dots as he lists the players. "The Federation has eighty-eight warships including five battlestations."

Turning to Lazarus, Corso said, "Your idea has merit but only if we use existing political lines. On one side is the Brotherhood and China. On the other is the North American Federation, the European Union, Japan, and India. As you say, we must invite them all to come out and play."

"We could be opening Pandora's Box. There's no controlling where this could lead," Councilor Debouch said.

Councilor Yang Lee frowns, "What you're advocating is mass murder."

"What we're *discussing* is our survival." Abby retorts.

"Global war will kill billions of innocent people." Councilor Yang Lee said. "Is our survival worth that?"

"That's the question, isn't it?" Abby replies. "Are we justified in killing others so that we may live? Evolution dictates only the strong survive to pass their genes on to the next generation. Have we evolved to the point that we can set aside nature's most basic law? I don't think so. Regardless, I'm not going down without a fight."

Before Abby's finished speaking, Councilor Yang Lee holds up his hands in surrender, "It seems my freehold citizens agree with you." Bowing his head, he vanishes.

Lunarian political system is very different from any that come before. Councilors have no set term of office. They serve for as long as they have political support. It's routine for the Council to see changes in personnel during a heated debate.

A petite oriental woman with raven black hair and a beautiful porcelain complexion appears in Yang Lee's place. The robes of office swirl about her. Her youthful features belie the maturity in her eyes.

"Greetings," she bows deeply, "I am Li Wei Chang, Councilor of the Hunan Freehold." The formal announcement was unnecessary. They all know who she is.

"Welcome back Li Wei," Abby said warmly, "I only wish it were under better circumstances."

"As do I Abigail. It is with deep regret that Hunan freehold aligns with this plan," Councilor Li said softly.

Abby lays out a poll, "I call on the Council to immediately initiate a mission to be known as Pandora. Its goal is to set up the conditions necessary to bring the other warlike nations into the fight if we choose to do it. The specifics are yet to be determined."

The tally is swift and overwhelming. The citizens of the Republic of Luna want to live.

"What about Al Fahad?" Councilor Hanley asks. "The invasion of our cities must have originated in Al Fahad."

"Nuke it." Councilor Johanson exclaims.

"Nuking Al Fahad would immediately bring retaliation." Councilor Taylor exclaims.

"Not if you do it right," Lazarus said. "Done right, it could have a profound effect on every Muslim in the empire."

Abby looks disgusted, "Do you really think that's necessary?"

Lazarus holds his ground. "Not for revenge, but for maximum effect. If you take out Al Fahad in the right way, you may end the war right there. The Army of Islam may lay down their arms and stop fighting."

"What do you mean, the right way?" Abby asks.

"There's only two things that can make a mujahedeen stop fighting, kill him or convince him that Allah wills it. Logic will not work and strength of arms simply forces him underground. We need to make it seem as if Allah disapproves of the actions taken by the Prince and his ministers," Lazarus said.

"Just how do you propose to do that?" Councilor Taylor asks.

"By preying on their religious superstitions. We must convince them that it's Allah's will… the mujahedeen will follow what they have been taught in the madrasa," Lazarus said.

"Dare I ask, what is a madrasa?" Councilor Taylor asks.

"A madrasa is a school that teaches fundamentalism. It's the only education most of them receive," Lazarus said.

"Why should I care about their schools?" Councilor Taylor asks.

"Understanding your enemy is the key to victory," Lazarus said.

"I ask again, why should I care where they go to school?" Councilor

Taylor asks sharply.

"As young boys, mujahedeen spend their youth just as their ancestors did, memorizing the Holy Qur'an. They learn to recite it back chapter and verse. It takes the average ten-year-old boy about three years. To make matters worse, they must memorize it in Arabic, but the boys come from every ethnic corner of the world. Some never learn Arabic beyond this rote memorization. The teachers read to them in Arabic and they recite it back for eight hours a day until they memorize the whole book."

"After graduation, the boys are enrolled in an eight-year course of study that focuses on the Holy Qur'an, and the Hadith. Most become mujahedeen, or soldiers, but a few of the more gifted will go on to become Mufti or Imam. Mufti sets social policy. Imam sets political policy. They are the leaders in Muslim society yet their education encompasses only theology, no world history, no math, no science, only a total immersion in fundamental Islam. Many brag that the Qur'an and Hadith are the only books they have ever read."

"How exactly do you propose we take advantage of this?" Councilor Taylor asks.

"Their unwavering belief makes them vulnerable. While it's an incredible force for controlling their army, staged in the right way, these soldiers can be influenced," Lazarus explains.

"What's the right way?" Councilor Taylor asks.

Seeing Lazarus hesitate, Abby steps in, "Lazarus doesn't need to give a detailed description at this time. We can all see advantages in the plan." Abby turns to him, "Lazarus, are you willing to work with Corso to come up with some ideas?" He nods, "Good. When you present them to the Council, we will decide which, if any, to go with."

Councilor Taylor visibly relaxes, "Very well, but I want all discussions to remain in public domain subject to the Law of Full Disclosure."

"Of course," Abby replies, "I wouldn't have it any other way."

Battle of Aldrin Station

Let those who would prefer the Hereafter to the Present life,
Fight in the cause of Allah. And who so Fights in the cause of
Allah and is Killed...We shall soon grant him a great Reward.

Holy Qur'an 4:74

Jordan and Jamie are strapping the figure to a seat in the back of the Moonhawk when Lazarus vidcasts next to them.

"Tempel is finishing prelaunch. Do you have any last thoughts before we send our messenger off?" Jordan asks Lazarus.

Lazarus shakes his head. "I understand enough to know you guys have exceeded my wildest imagination."

Jamie looks intently at him, "Don't be so modest. We couldn't have conceived of this without you."

"Explain to me again, what's a dPhag?" Lazarus requests.

"dPhag stands for Dimensional Phase Generator," Jamie said patiently.

"When enough energy is concentrated in a Calconn coil, space warps and a small black hole is created," Jordan said.

"Black holes link our universe to the next within the Superverse. The hole's we create are not very large, about the size of a proton, but when you super-energize the millions of micro-coils in a ghost suit, it phases into the next universe," Jamie explains.

"I'm fuzzy on this Superverse thing," Lazarus said.

Jamie smiles, "I assure you, the dPhag is essential for your plan to work."

"It's the key bit of technology that puts this mission over the top," Jordan adds.

"We've never tested it at this scale," Jamie adds.

"But we're sure it will work," Jordan adds.

"But if you've never done it before, why are you so sure it will work?" Lazarus asks.

"Magi's theoretical calculations are very accurate," Jamie replies.

"She never makes a mistake," Jordan adds.

"Time to roll," Tempel said.

"I still think I should be going with you," Lazarus moves up the aisle towards Tempel nodding to the warriors aboard the Moonhawk. He's getting better at vidcasting.

"The decision's made," Tempel replies.

"Tempel, you don't realize what effect that thing back there will have on the Brotherhood. Some of them will want to stop fighting. Give them a chance but don't expose yourself. They can revert back to violence at any time." He leans down to look the young Lunarian in the face. "If you need to fight then take it to them Tempel, just like you did in Nell's Valley. You hear me. Give 'em hell."

"**Give 'em hell**," Jordan and Jamie echo.

"*Aye,*" Quan Kiai said.

"Heaven's what they're expecting but it's hell we're bringing." Corazon is trying to sound like Brice and failing miserably but they all appreciate his effort.

Tempel looks intently at Lazarus and said dryly, "I'll give them your message."

Jordan follows Jamie down the ramp and it shuts behind them.

Lazarus stands alone watching the Moonhawk rise from the floor of the hanger at Miller's Farm. A crew had just finished stealth coating their Moonhawk and is now working on the other. The non-reflective surface makes the ship a shadow among shadows long before it reaches the farm's access tunnel. Within seconds, it's gone. *I hate waiting.*

ЯL

The city's massive atmospheric circulators are silent and the sky is dark. Hundreds of small fires flicker across the devastated commonway. Smoke fills the still air so thick in places that sensors cannot penetrate. The temperature is over 50°C.

The Brotherhood selected well. Their camp is at the top of Serenity Hill, a flat-topped mesa about twenty meters above the surrounding commonway. The great tunnel is wider here. The east/west slidewalks weave around the base of the hill. Stripped of its majestic oak trees, convoys crowd Serenity's summit, their thick armor bristling with cannon. In the flickering light, it looks like a medieval castle.

Lieutenant Taylor scampers through this hellish environment harassing the enemy that has invaded his home. Others are doing the same, making it impossible for the Brotherhood to relax.

The warriors are playing a dangerous game, ignoring the invaders incessant demand to cease-fire or die in a nuclear holocaust. To Taylor's left is what appears to be a group of Lunarians operating a heavy disrupter. Tucked in behind a massive piece of fire-blackened hardwood, it methodically pulses powerful beams across the intervening space. Another almost identical emplacement sits fifty meters beyond it and slightly forward. It too keeps constant pressure on the enemy encampment. The thunder of each discharge echoes down the immense stone passageway. In return, they have received an inordinate amount of attention from Brotherhood gunners. After all, they are immobile while the warriors are shadows on a dark night and much harder to hit. The Lunarian battlefield technicians have lost count how many times they have repaired the emplacements, getting them back up and firing within minutes.

71

Even as Taylor watches, another warrior, having exposed himself while making some imaginary adjustment to the weapon, takes a hit to his chest and falls back, apparently dead. It bothers Taylor even though he knows it's only a computer-generated illusion. The warrior is not real. None of the Lunarians operating these emplacements are flesh and blood. They serve only to encourage the invaders to think they are inflicting more casualties upon the infidels than they really are. The deception is a central feature of the plan to maintain pressure while cultivating the misconception that the Brotherhood soldiers are holding their own.

Lieutenant Taylor and his warriors are very much a part of this perilous ploy, exposing themselves, even if only briefly, as they fire at the enemy. Tiny spybots seek out and mark the location of every enemy combatant. The devices are small, numerous, and hard to detect. Magi prioritizes the targets and feeds the fire control data to the appropriate warrior. All they need do is look and fire, thus limiting their exposure. The resulting enemy attrition is high, and even with the elaborate deception, the Brotherhood will soon fall back to lick their wounds. No fighting force can withstand such losses for long.

Oak Ridge and Sherwood Forest commonways are the two fronts of the invaders campaign. Corso estimates they are facing about eighteen thousand troops in Sherwood and another twenty thousand in Oak Ridge but those numbers are dropping rapidly. Spybots have verified the locations of both nukes. Corso sets in motion a plan to eliminate them.

Behind Lieutenant Taylor, hidden around a bend in the commonway, the Lunarians release a swarm of several thousand small flying devices, each the spitting image of a honeybee. The constant pressure of the attacks keeps the Brotherhood soldiers too busy staying alive to think it odd that a honeybee could survive this heat.

Some bees stay close to the ground amidst the rubble while others zoom high and come down on their target. The swarm converges on a troop carrier with the big Red Crescent on its side. The growing assemblage finally attracts the attention of a technician within the command center.

"*Sir. I am picking up something within our perimeter.*" Havildar Ezzedine said in Arabic.

The bees now cover a spot almost a meter wide on the undercarriage of the massive vehicle, their energy signature partially obscured in its shadow. Once in place, these bees do not move like their biological counterparts, crawling and squirming over one another. Instead, they pack together and remain motionless, building up like a tumor on the carrier's belly, waiting patiently for the signal that will complete their mission.

"*What is it Havildar?*" Imam Bakr asks. He walks over to stand behind the man looking over his shoulder at the screen.

Lieutenant Taylor leads his warriors away from the battle lines, slinking through the debris and disappearing into a small opening in the side of the massive passageway. The warrior's pace is fast. They know what's coming. One by one, the frontline Lunarian companies declare that they are clear.

Even as Imam Bakr watches, the last of the strange energy sources settles on the hospital carrier and grows silent. His heart races as he recognizes danger.

Moments after the last Lunarian unit reports in, the order goes out to both Oak Ridge and Sherwood Forest. Within a nanosecond of each other, the bees explode. Each swarm totals almost three kilos of SuperX, the most powerful chemical explosive ever devised by man. The thick metal vaporizes along with the nuclear device hiding just beyond. The blast surges upward killing everyone onboard. It rips the thick armor as if it were tissue paper and picks up the mangled vehicle, dropping it on the adjacent troop carrier. Atomized uranium blankets Serenity Hill and beyond.

The news of the success spreads quickly through the city. Lieutenant Taylor smiles grimly watching his warriors whoop and holler with excitement even as they prepare to finish the job.

Cris wakes with a start. He lies there for a moment, unsure what had awakened him. Then he hears it, the distant thunder of explosions.

He looks around the small room. Where was Callie? She had been here when he fell asleep. He shakes his head. She was a big girl and fully capable of taking care of herself but it bothered him.

Rolling out of bed, he pulls on his freshly cleaned vacsuit in record time. The battle is a constant rumble and getting louder. Explosions shake the mountain around him sending bits of dust floating softly to the floor. With his pistol at his waist and the sword across his back, Cris heads towards the sound.

The tunnel outside the room is clear as far as he can see. The sounds are coming from only one direction. He leans forward and leaps, his body flexing into motion as easily as making a fist. A Highlander at full speed is something to behold out on the surface. Here, in the narrow confines within Ransburg, it's astonishing. With grace born of skill and practice, Cris uses every surface as he races through the twisting tunnels towards the battle.

Cris bursts into the cavern. This isn't an open space like those in Aldrin Station. The miners chased the ore deposits creating a hodgepodge of interconnected rooms and galleries. A mini rocket detonates next to Cris knocking him off his feet but he quickly regains control and keeps moving. Electromagnetic hardening of his vacsuit at the shrapnel's points of impact protects him.

A dozen more of the deadly little missiles, streak towards him from out of the labyrinth. Cris fires repeatedly, vaporizing them before they get close. He climbs up the side of a stone column and looks ahead. A large force of Brotherhood soldiers are forcing Conrad and what's left of his squad to fall back. Two warriors lie dead and many more are missing. They are losing the battle.

Cris cuts across ducking into a side tunnel and heading up a ramp. Racing upward, he twists through the tight turns and emerges back into the cavern far above the floor. He leaps from one dubious handhold to the next, circling the room. Like an avenging angel of death, Cris drops down among the Brotherhood soldiers from above, his pistol in one hand and the sword in the other.

He's a hawk among doves, delivering death surely and swiftly. Nothing can stand against him. Thrust with one hand, aim and fire with the other, then on to the next two targets at a speed that no earthborn human could ever hope to match. Cris cuts and blasts a swath through the soldiers like a scythe cutting hay. Blood runs in rivers across the stone floor. His pistol scarcely has time to recharge before thunderously firing again and his sword never stops moving.

Cris is a blur within the dim confines of the subterranean mining town, leaving a trail of dead Brotherhood soldiers behind him. They cannot stop what they cannot see. Terrified men blaze away at shadows only to die an instant later. The battle rages on until those still alive turn and run with Cris in close pursuit. They are even easier to kill from behind.

$$\mathcal{RL}$$

The force of the blast rocks the Goliath, throwing around the men inside as if they were rag dolls. Imam Bakr picks himself up off the floor. Around him, the members of his senior staff regroup. Several are injured and one is unconscious, his head bleeding profusely.

"*Havildar Ezzedine, report. What just happened?*" Imam Bakr demands. He wipes away blood from a cut lip with the back of his hand.

Havildar Ezzedine was the only person strapped into his seat when the explosion occurred. "*Sir, the point of origin was the hospital. It is destroyed. No survivors. Sir, why did they attack our hospital?*"

"*Because they are Djinn.*" Imam Bakr said bitterly, knowing the real reason. He's staring failure square in the face. Without the nuke buried in the bowels of that hospital to keep the Lunarian horde at bay, it's only a matter of time before all is lost. How could they have possibly known where the nuke was? These mutants are the flatulence of Satan.

Imam Bakr immediately begins to organize what's left of his army for a hasty retreat, knowing they would need to fight their way out of the city. He initiates a call through the secure relays they have placed between the two forces.

Twenty kilometers away as the crow flies, if a crow could fly through solid stone, Malik said to the call. His face is a strange mixture of dread and anger, "*Imam?*"

"*Do you still have your bomb?*"

"*No,*" Malik shakes his head. "*The infidels have destroyed it.*"

"*Mine is gone as well. We must abandon the city,*" Imam Bakr said.

Malik scowls in disgust, "*I do not like retreating.*"

"*Do you like dying?*" Imam Bakr replies sharply, "*Or perhaps you intend to surrender?*" The Imam smiles at the anger that flushes Malik's face. "*This is not the Lunarian General Council, Captain Malik. We are not discussing this. I have made my decision. Prepare your men for fighting because I do not believe the infidels will simply let us leave. You must move as quickly as possible before they have time to gather their strength. By the grace of Allah, we will leave this accursed place before the infidels know we are gone.*"

"*As you command, Imam. Where do we meet?*" Malik asks.

"*You have the shorter route back through Sherwood Commonway.*

Once you are on the surface, do not wait for me, Lieutenant. Take your men to Purgatory. We will regroup there." Imam Bakr is not at all confident that he will ever see the light of day again.

"*As you command,*" Malik growls.

"*Allah Akbar,*" Imam Bakr bows his head.

"*Allah Akbar.*" Malik replies and breaks the link.

Imam Bakr's swift decision is the only thing that saves his army. It surprises the Lunarians by its suddenness. Within minutes of the destruction of the nuke, both detachments are moving back the way they had come.

Most of the common soldiers do not have the scientific training to realize the danger inherent in radioactive fallout. It is simply dust clinging to their battle armor. However, their officers know. Those soldiers closest to the blast but still able to fight will lead them out of the city. Soldiers too badly injured are administered poisons that stop their hearts. To them, it seems a very humane way of dealing with their wounded. They're better dead than in the hands of the infidels.

The retreating Brotherhood is demoralized. Fear permeates the ranks at the realization that somehow, they have failed. Not even Allah can help them here in the heart of the infidel's city. Satan himself seems to be bearing down on them.

An explosion rocks the Goliath carrying Imam Bakr. Ahead of him, he can see the hell the lead convoys are going through. Beams mercilessly cut at the heavy vehicles. The commonway is awash in energy as the Brotherhood fights its way past a particularly difficult section. Shadowy figures flitter about in the dense smoke spreading death and destruction. A massive explosion rips through a Goliath. Imam Bakr silently watches the mad scramble as the undamaged troop carriers it was towing shift to other Goliaths, all done in the midst of a fierce firefight.

He addresses a convoy commander, "*Colonel, send 107 and 113 to attack along the right wall. We must break through the infidels if we are to live."*

The Imam tries to remain calm but he knows how precarious the next few minutes will be. *"Get us out of this accursed hole."* he commands even as the vehicles lurch forward gaining speed, heading directly for the Lunarians. The Brotherhood must blast their way past if they have any hope of breaking free.

The air is dense with smoke and if his battle helmet had not protected his ears, he would be deaf from the beam induced pressure waves that roil the commonway. What's left of his command is moving forward, weaving through the fallen trees.

The retreat takes far less time than the initial attack. Speed is of utmost importance. Anything that slows them down increases the likelihood that no one will make it out alive. Several convoys are abandoned, the soldiers inside left to the mercy of the Lunarians.

As he disappears into the dense smoke, Imam Bakr reminds these unlucky souls of the riches awaiting those who fight and die in the cause of Allah.

The minutes drag until they finally come to the end of Oak Ridge Commonway. Imam Bakr praises merciful Allah. The main airlock is only a little further. The air is motionless, the last fighting at least a kilometer to his rear.

For the first time since this started, Imam Bakr has hope that he will see the surface once more. He takes stock of what remains of his army. Of the twenty thousand soldiers he started with, less than three thousand make it out alive.

The Messenger

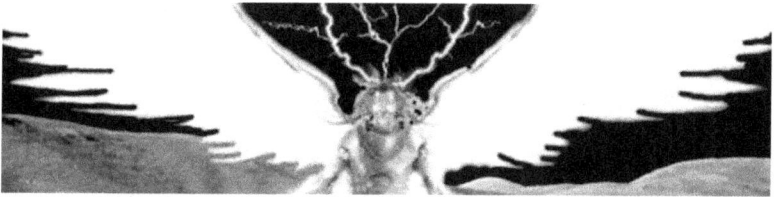

*And the fifth angel sounded and I saw a star fall from heaven
unto the earth and to him was given the key of the bottomless
pit. And he opened the bottomless pit and there arose a smoke
out of the pit, as smoke of a great furnace, and the sun and the
air were darkened...*

Holy Bible, Revelations 9:1-2

The shadowy figure creeps forward, its sensors sweeping up and
down the electromagnetic spectrum looking for the slightest hint of
danger. It's taking advantage of a small rill to get as close to Al Fahad
as possible.

The reserve element of the Army of Islam is preparing to march.
Dozens upon dozens of convoys stretch out side-by-side across the
landscape. Tankers filled with hypergolic fuel are further out. Armed
rovers scurry about the perimeter. No one notices when a section of the
outer fence flickers for a few seconds.

The figure keeps to the rill and gets within a half kilometer of the
city's main entrance. Rising up, it strolls boldly between rows of troop
carriers towards the front of the convoys. It releases a small spybot

which lands on the top of one of the nearby carriers giving it a good field of view for what was about to happen.

The figure transmits a laser signal. An instant later, every antenna in the Four Craters Region transmits maximum energy at the first of sixty-five sources of the jamming, overloading and burning them out, one after the other. Moments after the last jammer goes down, a patchwork constellation of communications satellites comes online. For the first time in more than three days, Earthnet is functional. When humanity realizes it's back online, they set the network ablaze.

The figure remains unchallenged. It emerges from between two convoys and approaches a lone Goliath. Plasma begins to flow from the stubby appendages across its back spreading out on each side of the figure like an angel's wings. A rover skids to a stop behind it. The figure leaps to the top of the Goliath. The alarm spreads.

Abby, Corso and most of Aldrin Station link with the spybot to witness realtime what was enfolding at Lassell crater. All across the Republic, citizens become aware of something unusual happening and join the link. However, the Lunarians are not the primary audience. The entirety of human space is receiving the broadcast, including the Islamic Brotherhood. The number of links quickly soars into the hundreds of millions then billions as humanity takes notice. The wings of the figure grow larger as more and more plasma races out along magnetic lines of force in a man-made aurora borealis. Energy ripples and flows across their expanse.

Supercharged electrostatic fields whip its long hair into frenzy. Its eyes flare, its wings grow, and still the intensity increases. Bolts of pure energy shoot from the figure forming a gigantic loop above its head. More and more energy fills the figure until it stares out at the world with eyes as bright as the sun.

It opens its mouth and broadcasts in perfect Arabic, "*Heed these words for they come from Allah.*" Energy streams from its mouth with every word. *"Cease this evil deed that is transpiring. For I, Archangel Gabriel, say unto all believers, this is an unjust jihad."*

Inside Al Fahad, Sheik Mohammad Abas is stunned. His brain can't cope with what he's seeing. This must be a trick. The infidels are behind this sorcery. They must be. He summons his lieutenants.

"What should we do?" Havildar Hassan Adawi asks. He's outside on the surface confronting the figure.

"Shoot it," Sheik Abas orders. When no one moves, he repeats louder and with more authority, *"Shoot it."* The frightened and confused look on the face of his lieutenant would be comical if it wasn't in such dire circumstance. *"Don't let the infidels fool you. This is just a cheap trick. I order you to shoot it. All of you. Every true believer that can hear my voice. Shoot it now."*

The apparition stands before them, not trying to flee or showing the least propensity in defending itself. It remains conveniently before the gunners.

Havildar Adawi tentatively fires his rover's laser cannon, striking the shimmering figure in the chest. Hesitantly at first, others open up. Within seconds, dozens of powerful weapons join in. The figure absorbs the onslaught, growing larger and brighter with every laser watt, sucking up exploding missiles like a black hole devouring a star.

The one sided battle escalates until the gunners begin to realize that their firepower is totally ineffective. In fact, the entity seems to be relishing the maelstrom, feeding upon it. One by one, the cannons shut down and the missiles stop coming. The figure stands before the Army of Islam, its great wings shimmering like the limbs of a mighty tree in a gale wind. It has the world's undivided attention.

"It is I who brought down this Qur'an on your heart by the command of Allah, which confirms the Scriptures that preceded it, and is a guidance and good tidings to the believers. Let him bear in mind that whoever is an enemy to Allah and His angels and His Messengers and Gabriel and

Michael, then, of course, Allah is an enemy to such disbelievers."

The angel's wings continue to grow larger and larger until they stretch over the entire compound, encompassing all beneath their fiery embrace.

"Behold the glory of Allah. For it is the leaders of this unjust war whom an evil reckoning awaits and their refuge is the Fire of Gehenna."

The great wings sweep over the gathering in sheets of fire. Energy ripples through the canopy. The Brotherhood cowers in fear below the shimmering expanse.

"What is happening," Sheik Abas demands. *"Mehmood. Tell me what is happening,"* He asked Mehmood Hussain, his chief scientist.

"I don't know..." Mehmood can't think clearly. He frowns and pulls in data to analyze but can only stare at the apparition.

"Archangel Gabriel is angry," someone exclaims.

"That is not Gabriel," Sheik Abas cries out but he's not so sure anymore.

The Messenger outshines the sun, spreading its wings over the entire army. The figure has become the center of a light show like no other in history. Energy pulsates across the vastness in complex patterns that seer themselves into the human collective, undulating across the wings in enormous waves, strobing faster with each passing second. The eyes of the human race are upon it.

"We shall cast into Fire all those who deny Our Message." The beat increases, *"As often as their skins are burnt up, we will replace them,"* faster and faster, *"with other new skins that they may continually taste the agony of punishment,"* the throbbing grows into a brain shattering strobe, *"Surely, Allah is All Mighty, All Wise."* It reaches a crescendo.

The apparition emits a final pulse of light a million times brighter than the sun then nothing. The feed from the spybot abruptly stops, cutting off the spectacle from humanities eager gaze. It takes precious seconds as technicians scramble to find other sensors and focus them on Al Fahad. What they find is astonishing. Where the horde of war machines had stood is now a huge hemispherical cavity many kilometers across and deep. The Brotherhood's military reserve and most of its anchor city have vanished along with millions of tons of lunar rock.

The void bites deep into the crater wall. Along the sheer cliff face, air and other gases leak out from what's left of the city but the discharge is pitifully small in the vast expanse of what's gone.

ЯL

General Arif is stunned. How can this be. He motions for the communications officer to replay the vid. No one on the bridge of the Houris has said a word. They sit at their stations and stare numbly at their screens, hands frozen over the controls. Shock rests on them like a dead weight. To a man they are convinced they had just witnessed a miracle, but one with confusing connotations. Several begin to chant, *"Allah Akbar. Allah Akbar."*

These men have spent a significant part of their lives studying the holy books of Islam. The angel spoke to them in the ancient tongue of the wrongness of the jihad they are waging, using passages almost verbatim from the Holy Qu'ran. Their education ruthlessly suppressed any desire to question authority, rooting out and dealing harshly with any freethinking. This reverberates not only through them, but into every corner of the Brotherhood. It's a body punch that threatens to stop the heart of an empire.

Al Fahad is gone. General Arif can detect no electronic signals from the city. With growing trepidation, he calls Imam Abu Bukhari. When the familiar face of the Imam appears, General Arif finds strength in his steady gaze. Imam Bukhari's words carry great weight.

"Allah be with you, my friend." Seeing panic in the general's eyes, he said, *"Do not be fooled by Satan's clever disguises. Be assured, our cause is just. We spread the message of the last prophet, peace be upon*

him. Allah has not forsaken us."

"Yes, of course Imam." General Arif replies shaken and unconvinced.

"I am assisting in the preparation of a general broadcast. Prince Al Zarqowi will address the Brotherhood within the hour." Imam Abu Bukhari shakes his head, *"It is a terrible thing that has happened, but sacrifices must be made when fighting the forces of evil. Do everything in your power to determine who is responsible for this atrocity and bring them to justice. Use your science and your brain. That is why Allah gave them to you. Let me know personally of your findings."*

"Yes, of course." General Arif replies bowing his head to the holy man.

"I am sorry but I must go. Remain steadfast in your faith, Salam." the Imam is one of the few who can call the general by his personal name. *"Allah Akbar."* he said as he bows and fades from view.

Anger grows until it overwhelms the fear and confusion. A man doesn't become the Major General in charge of the biggest conflict in Islamic history by being gullible. General Arif is a curious combination of modern science and religious fundamentalism. His study of science has shown him many things that could have shaken his belief in Allah, and did for many others. But he has always had the ability to fall back on the teachings of his childhood, his personal relationship with Allah and the Prophet Muhammad (*peace be upon him*). He believed in the righteousness of the cause while tempering it with a harsh dose of reality. When he thought of it at all, he thought of it as the economics of survival, contorting his beliefs to encompass the facts, ignoring the pieces that simply wouldn't fit. As he emerges from the fog, his mind reaches the same conclusion as the Imam, refusing to accept what he had seen at face value.

Of course, Imam Bukhari is right. It must be a trick. Allah would not forsake his loyal followers but it's hard to get past even for Major General Arif, Supreme Commander of the Islamic Expeditionary Forces.

"Admiral Alsamh. Find out what that was." General Arif commands.

High Admiral Rasheed Abou-Alsamh is a single rank below General Arif and second in command aboard the Houris. As a devout Muslim, he said his five daily prayers, fasts, gives generously to charity, and has twice made the Hajj. For the first time in his life, doubt clouds his mind. He can't rid himself of the image of the Archangel. Uncertainty burns like wildfire within his beliefs.

Nevertheless, he's a bridge officer, *"As you will."* Turning to his science officer, a man he has known and trusted for over a decade, *"Doctor."* the man didn't hear him, *"Doctor."* he said louder.

Dr. Saleh Al-Wohaiby is the Sub-Minister of Science for the fleet and has been on General Arif's staff from the first day he accepted command. He turns to face the Admiral in shocked disbelief. Slowly, visibly, the man pulls himself together.

"Yes Admiral," he said after a few seconds.

"Do a full analysis on the entity from the moment it arrived to the detonation. I want to know how it got there, where it came from, and where it went. And Saleh... if I have forgotten anything, do those tests as well. You know the drill. Let's find out what that thing was."

The doctor is dazed, *"What if it is as it seems?"*

Gripping the man by the shoulder, he looks intently into his eyes, *"Start your tests Saleh. Find out what you can."*

"Yes... Yes of course. Tests..." he looks back down at his control panel and slowly reaches out. It will take time for him to gather himself to the point of becoming useful again but at least he's moving.

Admiral Alsamh signals across the void to the frigate Hamas, *"Captain Shaikh."* When the man appears before him, his appearance is drawn. He too is under pressure and struggling to maintain composure.

"Yes Admiral," the man said tentatively.

"You are to immediately proceed at full speed to Al Fahad. You will be our eyes and ears on the ground. Do you understand?"

Captain Shaikh stares blankly back at him for a moment. The Admiral can see the fear build as the order sinks in.

"*Perhaps another would be better for this assignment. I am but a humble servant of Allah.*" Lieutenant Shaikh stammers dropping his gaze from the Admirals.

Admiral Alsamh can't believe his ears. Never has a captain of a ship in the fleet questioned an order, let alone refused one. He must put a stop to this immediately or lose control of his command.

"*Captain.*" the admiral growls, "*You will do as ordered or suffer the consequences.*" That's a death sentence for an officer having reached this level of responsibility.

The captain still wavers, looking around like a cornered animal. He finally nods. "*I will leave immediately.*"

Major General Arif settles back in his command seat, letting his subordinates perform their duties as he watches and listens, tuning in to various channels scattered across the fleet. He's only beginning to realize the magnitude of what's happened.

$$\mathcal{RL}$$

A spybot stumbles on the convoy by accident. From a thousand meters up, it looks normal enough but they can detect no light, no heat, no emissions at all from the vehicles. Sinking lower, the bot encounters a fog of death hanging heavy upon them. People had died here, in numbers.

"There's no damage that I can see," Sam said.

"Where are the bodies?" Tempel asks.

"We need to send someone in," Tatiana said. "Let me take Marcel and go find out what happened."

"No," Tempel said. "I'll go… Kipper, you're with me," Tempel unbuckles his harness.

"You're the Captain now. You're supposed to lead from the rear. Let me do my job," Tatiana said.

Tempel glances at her, "Don't worry, you'll get your chance. Right now, I want to see what happened out there." He slings a forensics kit over his shoulder and cinches it down around his waist.

"It might be a trap," Corazon said.

"Might be," Tempel replies as he leads Kipper down the ramp. They leap into the night straight up the steep mountainside. The warriors relish the exertion. Agile as cats on a hot tin roof, they run along the ridge for a ways. On the roadway far below is the Brotherhood convoy, lined up as if they had just pulled over and stopped.

The two warriors descend from the heights and head straight for the lead Goliath. The unit commander would be there or in one of the nearby troop carriers.

Tempel motions for Kipper to hold. Cautiously, he moves in and opens the outer airlock door. He glances up and down the row of vehicles and back at Kipper before entering.

Inside the airlock, he turns the handle and pushes on the inner door. It swings open easily. The air is gone from inside and it's shrouded in darkness, not even a stray thermal signature to light his way. Tempel turns on his belt light, his hand resting on his pistol.

Vacuum mummified bodies litter the interior. They had collapsed where they stood so it must have happened fast.

"They're all dead," Tempel said. He rummages through the dead looking at their uniforms. He finds a body with a general's insignia. Two stars inside the crescent. Someone had shot him in the head, small caliber, close range.

Tempel pulls a DNA sampler from his kit and takes a few cells from the general and those around him.

"I'm going inside the next carrier," Kipper said.

Once inside, Kipper finds more dead soldiers. Some are in their bunks, others on the floor and one shriveled up corpse is sitting at a table like he's waiting for dinner.

"They're all dead," Kipper reports.

"Can you establish a cause of death?" Tempel asks.

"Explosive asphyxiation followed by vacuum dehydration is what it looks like. Someone opened the troop carriers to vacuum and killed them all."

"Same here with one exception. Somebody shot the general. I'm taking the Goliath's AI. Maybe it can tell us what happened." Tempel pulls the black case from its rack.

Tempel and Kipper look inside carrier after carrier. They're all the same. He estimates there were about a thousand soldiers in the convoy. They're all dead.

ℛℒ

Malik's close involvement with the Lunarians over the last several years has given him a deep appreciation of their cunning and technical abilities. After reviewing the vid yet again, he assures himself that it must be a trick of some kind, though he doesn't have the foggiest idea how they did it.

Even if he was inclined to share his conclusion, which he isn't, there are few around him that would give it any credence. The events of the day are simply too much for a simple mujahedeen. To the vast majority, they had witnessed a miracle, one that condemned them to hell.

Malik cursed this forsaken land and the people in it. He slaps his hand against the side of the Goliath. He yearns for the hot sands of Saudi Arabia, where a man didn't worry about his next breath and his enemies fought like men.

If it's war these godless Lunarians want, then it's war he will grant them.

ℛℒ

Magi interrupts, "Excuse me Lazarus, Abby requests a word with you,"

"Of course…" Lazarus looks up at her image standing on the other side of the table, "Greetings Abby."

"Greetings Lazarus. Sorry about the interruption. What are you having? It smells divine," Abby said.

"Soy sausage, biscuits and gravy, fried potatoes and orange juice. Liz has plenty. Would you like to join me?" Lazarus asks.

"That sounds marvelous. Nobody makes gravy like Liz. Maybe next time," Abby sighs. "I want to express my personal congratulations on the Al Fahad mission. Jason and Jamie tell me you were instrumental in designing the Messenger."

"Thanks, but I have no clue how they did that. Now we wait to see what happens. It shouldn't take long," Lazarus said.

"I'll let you get back to your breakfast, but as soon as you're finished, there are some things I would like to discuss with you."

"Sure. Give me five minutes," Lazarus said.

Abby looks tired. "Take ten and enjoy your food." She nods and disappears.

Liz comes over and sits beside Lazarus. "I wish she wouldn't work so hard. It's wearing her down."

"She takes her job very seriously," Lazarus said.

"She's carrying a tremendous load. It's worse than I've ever seen it, even for her." Liz shakes her head.

"These are tough times and someone must take responsibility. Abby handles it better than I ever could." Lazarus takes a bite. "How does a ninety-three year old woman look and act thirty-five?"

Liz pauses and looks intently at Lazarus. "You really don't know?"

His next bite stops halfway to his mouth. "Know what?"

His polygraphic indicators show he's not lying. "We've found a way to repair the damage done by aging," Liz said.

Lazarus takes the bite and stares at Liz as he chews. "She's immortal?"

"Heaven's no. Aging is a deterioration process that occurs over time. Every so often we simply restore our bodies to a state of good health," Liz said.

From somewhere behind them a voice said, "Greetings Liz. Could you spare another plate of biscuits and gravy?" Abby walks through the kitchen to their table.

"Abby." Liz jumps up and gives her a hug. "You look exhausted."

"Right now I could use some of your cooking." Abby turns to Lazarus admiring his new haircut, shaved right down to the nub, "I changed my mind. May I join you?"

"Of course... It's a woman's prerogative to change her mind. I'm glad you did." Lazarus stands while she sits.

"You're curious about why I look so young," Abby said.

Lazarus nods, "Aye."

"As Liz said, we've found a way to repair our bodies."

"Would you mind if I took off my visor?" Lazarus asks.

"Are you sure you're not from Missouri?" When Lazarus looks puzzled, Abby smiles, "I was born and raised in Missouri. It was called the *Show Me* state back then... By all means, let's both take our visors off." She lays her visor on the table just as Liz places a plate heaped with biscuits smothered in thick white gravy in front of her.

"There's plenty more," Liz said.

"There always is when you're cooking," Abby said. "Join us?" She pats the seat next to her.

Lazarus lays his visor next to Abby's and stares at her for several moments. Her long blond hair is loose this morning and ripples strangely in Luna's gravity when she moves her head. It's something only a shortimer would notice. However, she looks just like the image in his visor. He can find no difference.

"Well?" She asked.

"You're beautiful," Lazarus stammers.

"Of course I am… Liz, could you pass the salt and pepper?" Abby looks back at Lazarus, "As soon as things calm down, you can study modern genetics. Liz or Tara can take you over to see what a regeneration tank looks like and explain how it works."

"It would be my pleasure," Liz said.

Abby pulls her hair back and deftly puts it into a ponytail. "Over the years, we have made some minor modifications in my DNA. Straightened my nose, changed my hair color, that sort of thing. So if you look at me back in '24… Well, let's just say I look different now…" Abby scoops up a generous bite. "Liz. This is exactly what I needed."

Liz grins.

Every year the Federation devotes major resources in fighting the War on Genetics or the Clone War as some call it. Lazarus had been a part of that effort, shutting down dealers, tracking down illegal labs, and convicting pushers. Abby's casual admission would have meant complete reeducation back in the Federation. Here, it was polite conversation around the kitchen table. Lazarus remains quiet but his polygraphic indicators betray his emotions.

"Why does that bother you," Abby said. She doesn't need her visor to see that it does.

Lazarus stares into her green eyes and tells the truth. "I have sent people to reeducation for what you just freely admitted."

"Have you? The Federation is so hypocritical. The wealthy overindulge in genetics but withhold it from everyone else." Abby scoops in another bite.

Lazarus frowns. Clearly, he disagrees. He runs his hand over his head forgetting for a moment that his hair is all gone.

"President John Paul is the biggest hypocrite of them all." Liz adds. "He's been using genetics for half a century while denying it to his fellow citizens."

"I met President John Paul once when I was a kid. It was in the White House after my father died…" Lazarus looks at Liz. "So you're saying that John Paul uses genetics?"

"John Paul is ninety-two years old. Put your visor back on and look at his most recent public appearance." Abby put on hers and links with him just as Magi starts the vid.

Lazarus does and watches the President making a speech at West Point in front of the cadets. The man could hardly walk to the podium under his own power, yet stood there and delivered a vigorous speech. He faltered towards the end but finished strong. His courage and tenacity made Lazarus want to stand up and cheer.

"That is his political persona. Magi, show him the September vid of John Paul," Abby orders. "This was recorded at the Royal Resort in Cancun just a few days after that speech."

West Point disappears and now Lazarus is riding in a cart across a golf course. It's dusky and getting darker by the second. The cart stops next to a tall wooden fence. There is a brief flurry as the person making the record climbs on top the cart and peers over the fence. A private pool is on the other side.

The sliding glass patio door opens across the way and lights come on around the pool. Several armed men dressed in black suits emerge and take positions around the patio. Three men in bathing suits and a covey of bikini-clad beauties follow them out. With a squeal, the young women run and jump into the water. Two of the men continue talking as they take a seat. A male servant sits drinks next to them. The third man lets one of the girls coax him towards the pool. He laughs and slips off her scanty top. She pulls away with a mischievous grin and dives into the pool. The man follows. Lazarus recognizes him.

"That's President John Paul," Abby said. He couldn't be more than thirty-five. "If you still have any doubt as to why he looks so young,

Magi has thousands of hours you can view."

"No, that's not necessary," Lazarus said. It's as if he's looking at a ghost from the past. "It'll be a cold day in hell before I doubt you again."

"Indeed." Abby frowns and looks down at the table. "Something's been bothering me that I need you to clear up…"

"Go on," Lazarus said.

"When you defected, how did you convince them to let you go to Athens?" Abby asks.

"My wife and I planned the trip two years before and I cleared it with Director Dempsey."

"I see… so you asked and they let you go?"

Lazarus shrugs, "Athens is a popular vacation spot."

"Magi, how did Lazarus manage to escape the Federation?"

"I helped the dear boy," she replies.

Lazarus stares at her in disbelief. "What do you mean? How?"

"You and your surrogate would never have made it past security at Gateway Airport if I hadn't intervened. DHS issued a last minute detention warrant to take you into custody. I changed the warrant and assigned a surveillance team instead. Once in Athens, I helped you lose the team and obtain a ticket to Heaven's Gate. I bumped Clark Hamlin from the flight and put you in a seat next to Lindsey. The rest she did on her own."

Lazarus stares at Magi, replaying the memories of that day. Was that why airport security had stopped him then let him go? Is that why they charged him with multiple counts of Earthnet security breach? Then it hit him. "The face on the screen, the one selling tickets to Heaven's Gate, it was you."

"Yes Lazarus," Magi said.

"Is there anything else you haven't told me?"

"Of course. I spend a lot of time deciding what not to tell you," Magi said. "It's very easy to overload humans with information."

"What's this about a surrogate?" Abby asks.

"They sent it over after my wife died," Lazarus said defensively.

"It was a companion android, Japanese Model 4000," Magi said, "The very latest tech."

"You had sex with a machine?" The way she said it condemned him to hell for all eternity.

"Well… when you say it that way, it sounds bad." Reality tilts around Lazarus. The Senior Analyst part of him wants to know how Magi infiltrated Earthnet so completely. Something's going on here that doesn't make sense.

"How many times?" Abby won't let it drop.

"Do we really need to talk about this?" Lazarus implores.

"Yes… we do," she insists.

Lazarus looks away, "I don't know exactly. It was a lot at first but not so much the past year. It's been months since the last time."

"Magi, what do you know about this?" Abby is not happy. Magi should have told her.

"Lazarus ejaculated four-hundred-fifty-nine times into the surrogate producing over twenty billion sperm."

"For what purpose?" Abby asks.

"Lazarus has a very rare DNA profile. It's defect free. He's the perfect male donor."

Lazarus can't believe his ears. "What? You're crazy."

"I beg your pardon?" Magi's unaccustomed to being called crazy. "My dear boy, there are four-thousand one-hundred and fifteen children conceived using your DNA… that I know of."

The feeling that comes over Lazarus as he processes this information goes far beyond horror. "What're you saying?" he stammers. "The Federation wanted my sperm and used the surrogate to get it?"

"Yes Lazarus," Magi acknowledges.

"Then the accident…" he can't finish.

Magi sadly shakes her head, "I'm so sorry Lazarus but it wasn't an accident," she said kindly. "Director Dempsey wanted their deaths to look like an accident and had his agents rig the traffic lights which resulted in your wife and daughters fatal car wreck."

Hate consumes Lazarus. ***"GOD DAMN HIM TO HELL."***

Two Minute War

"War is a poor chisel to carve out tomorrow."

Martin Luther King, Jr. (1929 - 1968)

It was only a twinkle, quickly gone. Lieutenant Gilmore isolated the brief flash of energy and analyzed. Only then did he raise the alarm.

"Sir. Sensors have picked up an energy release." The lieutenant routes his findings onto the DAC's main display. The anomaly was over a hundred thousand kilometers away.

"What's your analysis, Lieutenant?" Admiral DyGoon asks.

"It's consistent with leakage from a missile launch, but I can't say for sure. We simply don't have enough information to make a call." The young officer said.

"Helm, take us to a higher orbit at best speed. Lieutenant Gilmore. Let's get some eyes out there, shall we. No need to guess." Admiral DyGoon orders.

"Yes sir." Lieutenant Gilmore said. He redirects several FOSATs towards the spot in space. The spybots streak across the void under constant acceleration. All but one decelerates to match orbital velocity. That one never slows down but sends back the first pictures as it races by.

There, floating in the silence of space is the unmistakable bulk of a battlestation. Its dark silhouette blocking out the stars betrays it as Brotherhood. A thick coating of energy absorbent material makes it invisible to anything except direct visual detection, and even then, it's only by its huge size blotting out the background stars that the FOSAT can detect it. It reflects no light, no heat, and no radar. It's a hole in space.

FBS Yorktown has been at full alert since the trouble began, every man at his battle station. Admiral DyGoon always errs on the side of caution.

As the Yorktown's thrusters push her into a new orbit, the space recently abandoned spikes with a great flash of energy. Alarms scream as radiation pounds the hull.

"Shields are up." Lieutenant Gilmore declares. The electromagnetic shields automatically respond to radiation at these levels. The rem count immediately drops inside the ship.

"Get us out of here helmsman." Admiral DyGoon orders.

"Sir. The helm is sluggish. Thrusters operating at only twelve percent." The young corpsman reports.

"Sir. The Brotherhood battlestation is coming about." Lieutenant Gilmore declares. It appears as if the giant ship is lining up for another shot.

"Missile battery Tango Six, prepare to fire." Admiral DyGoon orders. Because of the shields, his ship is now lit up like a spotlight on a moonless night but he can't drop them until the radiation falls. That will take another thirty minutes at least. What's worse, it takes time for the Calconn circuitry in his megathrusters to recover from a point-blank nuclear EMP. He can't move.

One by one in rapid succession, their FOSATs stop sending data and the image of the battlestation grows blurry then disappears. The bridge crew scrambles to find another FOSAT but the nearest is almost thirty thousand kilometers away. The admiral can no longer see his enemy.

"Lieutenant Lutchi. Do you have lock on their last position?" Admiral DyGoon asks the weapons officer in command of Tango Six.

"Yes sir."

"Fire three in standard pattern, last known coordinates," Admiral DyGoon orders. He must act quickly before the battlestation disappears into the void.

Missiles leap from electromagnetic railguns at 30,000 Gs heading straight for a spot in space over a hundred-thousand kilometers distant. They use brute force to get there as the crow flies. Their onboard thrusters maintain two-hundred Gs all the way to the target.

The battlestation had accelerated away from the initial point of contact but not far enough. Two missiles detonate within a kilometer, the third within a hundred meters.

The tremendous burst of raw energy overwhelms the thick coating covering the battlestation. It glows red then white as it turns to ash and ablates, coming apart at the molecular level. It blows off in a dense cloud. Below it, the metal skin of the great ship is exposed. It too heats up, boiling away in the intense energy.

The blast peels the battlestation like a gigantic onion. Those outermost layers closest to the epicenter evaporate. Radiation kills most of the crew outright but a few survive. For those, death will take longer to arrive, but it will without exception.

Like a comet's tail, a stream of particles trail away from the stricken ship. With a great hole blasted in its side, the giant battlestation is adrift in space, its crew dead or dying. The Brotherhood fleet attacks the only Federation ship they can clearly see, the FBS Yorktown.

It's impossible to move the Yorktown fast enough to evade the incoming missiles. The ship's first line of defense is long-range laser cannons. They begin to fire but maintaining lock on a target accelerating at two-hundred Gs is close to impossible. They manage to hit only a few.

The second defensive layer is kinetic in nature. Railguns firing over four thousand rounds a minute target points in space where the AI calculates the trajectories will meet. The missiles avoid them easily, exploding just before impact with the hull of the Yorktown. The combined force of the blasts rips apart the huge battlestation killing everyone aboard. A scorched flotilla of metal fragments is all that remains of the once mighty warship.

The loss of the FBS Yorktown and Admiral DyGoon, ripples across the Federation fleet like a boulder dropped in a quiet pond.

"Theater wide orders. Implement plan Delta Six. I repeat, implement plan Delta Six." Rear Admiral Thomas Tyler is next in the chain of command. Admiral DyGoon had been a fine officer and a good friend but he would have been the first to tell him not to waste time mourning his death. Admiral Tyler's first command places the fleet on War Status.

FOSATs streak across orbits, searching in a vast grid. Warships maneuver randomly in an attempt to keep the enemy confused. Everyone's doing the same thing. Hundreds of ships are in motion.

A mine takes out an EU frigate. A few minutes later, a missile cripples India's only heavy cruiser. All across orbital space, fighters and missiles seek out targets. Mother Earth's orbit is quickly becoming history's largest battlefield.

"Sir. The Reagan is under attack." Lieutenant Morrison exclaims. He puts the feed from one of their FOSATs on the main screen. Swarming around the battlestation are hundreds of space fighters. Explosions flare and fade like fireflies across its surface. A nearby frigate takes a severe hit and limps off trailing gas. The FBS Ronald Reagan begins to break up right before their eyes. Fires and explosions rock the giant warship and the aft section spins off into the void.

First the Yorktown and now the Ronald Reagan are gone, two of the Federation's finest battlestations. Admiral Tyler reacts. "Fire at will. All hands, fire at will." The order goes out to the fleet.

"Lieutenant, launch all fighters. I want a shield around us that a fly couldn't get through," Admiral Tyler commands.

"Yes sir." He orders the first of many squadrons of space fighters into action. The battlestation quivers like a wild beast as each fighter group launches.

Flight Leader Tommy Thompson has two years experience flying a Centaur space fighter. He had asked for and received permission to lead the counterattack but it was the skill of the other pilots in his squadron as much as his leadership abilities that won the honor.

"OK meatheads. Let's get it done," Thompson growls. It's hard to believe the Yorktown and Reagan are gone. He had served on the Yorktown prior to his current assignment on the John Paul. Many of his closest friends are now space debris.

The squadron stays in loose formation, far enough apart to make it difficult to take them out with a single blow. After an initial high gee boost, they let Earth's gravity pull them around the planet towards their intended target so as not to give their position away.

ℛℒ

Purgatory looks almost peaceful from this distance. It could be a typical day in the life of the mining community. Closer inspection reveals wreckage strewn about the town's main entrance.

Malik doesn't stop to take in the view. He orders his forward elements to attack.

Missiles streak towards the massive airlock door. The thick steel disintegrates under the onslaught. More missiles streak past the shattered door seeking their next target, the inner airlock door. It too succumbs to the relentless assault, as does the next, and the next.

A dozen Goliath's follow close behind, taking the fight to the Lunarians. Within minutes, they breach the town's main hanger complex and are inside.

Malik directs several of the deadly killing machines to concentrate their firepower on the back wall. He's been inside Purgatory many times. He knows where it's most vulnerable. They blast a crude tunnel into the wall. With a tremendous burst, the last vestige of stone collapses and the town's air spews forth. Before the dust settles, he orders his soldiers into the breach. Once inside, they leave nothing untouched.

The fighting continues unabated until the last Lunarian citizen is killed or has fled. Imam Bakr commands them to take what they need from the ruins of the town. It's time to move on. Darpur is his next target. He will make these godless heathens pay for Al Fahad.

ℛ𝕃

Tempel pilots the Moonhawk over the desolate landscape keeping low. He nudges the flight stick occasionally, letting the AI do most of the flying. Sam, his copilot, sits to his right. The other Highlanders and the Moonhawk itself are invisible, filtered out by his visor. He and Sam appear to be alone soaring across the face of their world.

Magi breaks communications silence and abruptly appears beside him, "Tempel, we have a situation," she said. "Stand by for Corso."

"Standing by," Tempel alerts Sam and the other Highlanders of the call. They immediately link in.

"The Brotherhood attacked Purgatory. It's bad... very bad. Those bastards killed everyone." Corso is angry. It was his decision to let Imam Bakr and his soldiers go free once he evicted them from Aldrin Station. He blames himself for what happened at Purgatory.

Quan Kiai is a few kilometers ahead of the retreating Brotherhood army, near the edge of the Sea of Clouds. They were keeping an eye on them but it looks like they're going home, or at least what was left of it. Cris had put the fear of Satan in them and the Messenger finished the job.

"You're the closest combat team. I want you to discontinue your current mission and find Imam Bakr," Corso orders.

Tempel frowns but said without hesitation. "Aye. What do you want us to do when we find him?"

"I want you to stop him," Corso rumbles in his deep voice. "Let me clarify that, I want you to stop him dead."

"Aye. And the soldiers with him?"

"The same..."

ℛL

The battlestation Shenyang intends to stay clear of the hostilities, moving well beyond the orbit of Luna. Her sister ships follow. China sees this war as inevitable, one crazy religion going after another. It's a war that will leave China in control of the entire planet if they play their cards right.

"Lieutenant, maintain this course. Captain Tseng, deploy another dozen FOSATs. I want to know what's happening in the lower orbits." Admiral Liu Jianchao is confident in his crew's abilities and the Shenyang is performing flawlessly.

"Yes Sir."

A proximity alarm sounds, jarring the admiral from his thoughts. Something's approaching very fast. Admiral Jianchao turns to his Captain. The great ship lurches beneath him.

"Defensive batteries are firing."

The device arrives and detonates. The twenty-megaton pulse of radiation overwhelms the ships shielding killing everyone instantly. A nanosecond later, the thermal energy of the detonation vaporizes the Shenyang's outer hull and rips deep into the massive ship. It turns the once mighty battlestation into a spinning hulk of twisted metal. Vapors and fragments form a cloud around her. The blast has reduced her orbital velocity below critical value. Earth begins to draw in what's left of the battlestation. Months later, the flaming remnants of this once proud ship will light up the night sky over the North Atlantic and hit with the force of a nuclear bomb.

ℛL

Tempel lowers the Moonhawk's ramp and the platoon gathers at its base. Most of them already have their Shoulder Mounted Gun Platforms cinched tight ready for combat. Zoey helps Tempel into his and Tatiana helps Sam with hers. Talk is subdued as they prepare for battle.

"The spybots report twenty two Goliaths and a hundred-thirty-six troop carriers, less than seven thousand troops," Corazon said.

"They'll need more," Marcel said.

"Not even a fair fight," Zoey adds.

While they're talking, Kipper and Tatiana incorporate the information into the battle simulator. A terrain map of the Brotherhood coming down the Trans Lunar Highway appears before them about waist high.

Tempel moves into the projection and takes a position alongside a long broad valley. "Here's what I propose… We use a spread formation and stop their forward momentum with a massive aerial assault on the front of the column. That should force them into a defensive position… here… Then we hit them with a power play. Tatiana, you will attack their line... here... That will weaken it allowing the rest of us to bust into their secondary. Once we're inside their formation, we take everything out. I don't want a man or machine left in one piece… You know the drill. Let's do this by the book. Any questions?" he waits a few seconds. "Good. Let's run through a complete simulation."

Quan Kiai plunges into a sophisticated game of team combat, a dose of virtual warfare that allows them to try out the battle plan before risking their lives. Fifteen minutes and several adjustments later, they're finished, having coordinated targets and responsibilities for the attack right down to what weapon to use in each instance. Time well spent.

They gather around Tempel one last time. He turns looking intently at each in turn. These are his friends, his comrades and some of them might not see daybreak. "We do this by the book. There's no place on a battlefield for sportsmanship. That line of thinking will get you killed. If you can get behind them, do it. If you can shoot first, do it. Find a weakness and exploit it with overwhelming force. Work as a team. Together we're strong."

They're all thinking the same thought, Tempel sounds just like Kitajima. It's strangely comforting.

Tempel leans forward and thrusts his fist upward, "Quan Kiai."

The others join him and their fists come together in a tight circle, "*QUAN KIAI.*"

The team breaks formation. They strap extra rockets across their backs before moving out in single file with Tempel leading. Even with the extra weight, the Highlanders race over the rugged terrain hardly slowing as they scamper up and down steep mountainsides and across valleys.

The enemy is making good time, keeping to the Trans Lunar Highway. This part of the highway passes down the center of a broad valley.

Tempel stops well out in front of the approaching Brotherhood. The lead vehicles are coming towards them at about fifty kph. The other convoys are spread out behind them for over ten kilometers. Along each side of the valley is a high ridgeline about a kilometer from the road. The broad flat valley will encourage the Brotherhood to circle the wagons, so to speak. Quan Kiai selected the battlefield well.

"We Ready?" Tempel asks.

"*Aye. Locked and Loaded,*" Quan Kiai replies.

"Let's roll," Tempel orders.

Half of Quan Kiai takes the south side of the valley, the other half the north.

Tempel counts down, "On my mark... three... two... one... Mark."

Each of the ten warriors launches several missiles almost straight up. The deadly little darts already know their assigned targets, allowing the Highlanders to fire and forget. The warriors spread out and speed up.

The missiles begin hitting well before the warriors reach their assigned attack positions. The effect is stunning. Explosions rip open the lead Goliath of the first convoy. The orderly formation breaks up. The valley is in chaos as the other convoys veer off the road and begin to form into a circle. Floodlights mounted on top of the troop carriers flash on, pushing back the darkness. It takes time for the convoys in the rear of the formation to catch up and complete the maneuver.

Quan Kiai sprints past the convoys, attacking from the shadows and keeping well away from the glaring light. They don't even stop when they reload their missile launchers, doing it at full speed time after time. Interspersed within the missile barrage, their laser cannons punch holes in the troop carriers seeking out vital spots and forcing everyone inside to suit up or die. They fire in bursts timing their attacks to make it hard for the Brotherhood to lock on any one of them.

To the Brotherhood, the attacks are coming out of the darkness without any discernible pattern. Their gunners fire at shadows. Pinned down in an exposed position, facing an invisible foe, the soldiers start making mistakes. Imam Bakr's convoy collides with another, disabling both. The Imam never makes it to the protected center of the formation. Missiles slam into his Goliath killing everyone aboard. What remains of his army obeys his last command and forms a rough defensive ring.

Quan Kiai encircles the makeshift camp, half going one way, the other half the other, racing around the circumference while staying out of the floodlights. Early in the battle, Tempel remotely flies the Moonhawk to a forward position, a place convenient for reloading.

The soldiers fought back but are hopelessly outclassed. It's grown men taking on a bunch of first graders, it's a pack of wolves bringing down a fawn, there's simply no contest. The battle is completely one-sided. The Brotherhood becomes weaker and the soldiers fewer in number with each passing second. It is a death of a thousand cuts and it goes on and on and on without end.

On a predetermined signal, Tatiana, Kipper, Samantha, Zoey

and Corazon concentrate their missiles into the carriers along the southwestern flank. The last floodlight goes dark plunging the makeshift camp and the valley into darkness.

Tempel, Karyl, Alonzo, Angel and Marcel attack the weakened perimeter in a direct frontal assault. Leaping over a gutted carrier, Tempel opens up with his laser on the approaching rovers. In a silent spectacle of death, hyperbolic fuels mix and self ignite sending fireballs bursting skyward. Around him, Quan Kiai begins to hunt.

The Lunarians begin the first of many sweeps through the interior of the formation killing and destroying everything in their path. Time after time, usually in pairs, the warriors return to the Moonhawk to reload then quickly rejoin the battle. The red fog of death lies thick over the valley as the one-sided contest wears on. The Highlanders are the shadow of death. They never stop moving, never hesitate, they kill without conscience like a wild beast.

The battle rages on with the Highlanders never taking a break, never slowing down. Their missiles long since expended, they fire their lasers as fast as they can recharge. The scene inside the defensive formation slowly grinds down to an inevitable conclusion. Brotherhood soldiers are no match for the Lunarians. None at all.

Inside the perimeter, Malik orders the last of the soldiers to fall back and protect his command post in the center of the ring.

Lasers punch holes in the last untouched troop carriers, seeking out the vulnerable fuel tanks. Silent explosions rock the valley as hypergolic liquids boil into vacuum and mix.

Malik barely escapes the destruction of his carrier and is one of the last alive. Exhausted, he staggers forward to stand in the middle of the compound. He fires his pulse rifle in an arc at nothing in particular, screaming in frustration. He cannot see his enemy. Yet, all around him, his command lay in ruins. Vacuum sucks the blood from the dead and more red gore seeps from the wreckage adding to the heavy haze that already hangs over the valley like a death shroud. Thirty meters away, he witnesses the last soldier fall. He is alone.

Zoey and Alonzo close in for the kill but Tempel stops them. He approaches Malik from the side.

"Malik." Tempel casts to him.

The directional finder in Malik's combat vacsuit tells him roughly the bearing of the voice. The man swings towards it peering intently into the darkness. He can't see anything.

"Who's there?" Malik calls out.

"It's the death you seek," Tempel growls back.

"I recognize that voice. You are the young dog that killed Jafa. What are you waiting for. Finish the job." Malik again fires his rifle in an arc, blasting away at nothing. Empty, he throws it to the ground. He stands defiant waiting for the end.

Tempel is less than ten meters from the man when Malik finally detects him, not by vision, but by the smudge of darkness moving towards him. Malik draws his pistol and fires.

ℛ𝕃

Flight Leader Tommy Thompson's fighter squadron coasts around the Earth conserving energy while sneaking up on the battlestation. The ship knows something is there but can't pinpoint what or where. Lasers reach out probing space. At the very last moment, the Centaurs light up their thrusters and streak the final few kilometers.

Thompson leads them in a strafing run towards their assigned target, the engine room. The massive megathrusters hide behind thick armor and run the length of the battlestation but their nozzles are exposed.

Flying in a tight V formation, the squadron rips deep into the aft section of the battlestation, breaching the hull and releasing the atmosphere inside. They occasionally hit something more volatile, leaving a path strewn with tremendous explosions amidst clouds of vaporized metal. The fast moving fighters overrun the battlestations defensive gun emplacements, concentrating their firepower on one megathruster.

"Maintain formation." Flight Leader Thompson calls out. He hugs the surface, following its curve, firing continuously. His top priority is always the next gun emplacement emerging over the horizon. "Let's keep it tight." Behind him, his squadron fires powerful lasers downward into the ship.

Eagle Seven, flown by Pilot Third Class Edward Bailey, drifts too far from the chosen path. With a suddenness characteristic of all warfare, the fighter vaporizes. One second the Centaur is there, the next it's a cloud of atoms drifting in the vacuum of space.

"Eagle Eight, tighten it up. Maintain formation another forty seconds." Thompson implores his pilots. He had lost count of the number of laser cannons he has destroyed, that would come later when Commander Kline held his after action debriefing session.

Thompson glances at the energy remaining in his fighter. It's almost half-gone. He continues to pour it on taking out everything that appears before him. It was his job to plow the path.

Eagle Four disappears in a cloud of vapor. On the other side of the formation, Eagle Five suffers the same fate. The squadron is still below the accepted attrition rate for this type of attack.

"Thirty seconds." Energy pours from the fighters in copious amounts, ripping into the battlestation. A path of destruction lay behind them, clearly marking their zigzag course across the surface of the giant warship.

Eagle Eight takes a hit and careens off into space. Another shot finishes the job.

"Assume formation alpha," Flight Leader Thompson orders. Following the next darting change in direction, the squadron forms into a snowplow shape with Eagle One anchoring the front and Eagle Six the back. With only four remaining Centaur's, the flight has just enough firepower to maintain their speed.

"Twenty seconds." Flight Leader Thompson misses and before he can correct his mistake, the Brotherhood cannon fires. Tommy's fighter evaporates in a puff of atomized particles, the cloud drifting onward under its own momentum.

Eagle Two takes it out, destroying the gun emplacement in a flash of white-hot energy. With only three fighters left, they must slow down or risk missing another gun. What's left of the squadron concentrates on delivering their energy onto the battlestation's megathruster. It sputters and loses power. They're having an effect.

With ten seconds of energy remaining, Eagle Six cuts a corner too close and clips an antenna. The fighter spins out of control, its thrusters trying vainly to right the craft. It smashes into a tower and explodes.

The last two pilots can hear the countdown as they concentrate on finishing the mission.

They slow even further, darting across the surface, concentrating their remaining energy on the giant ship. Gasses explode in great geysers. They dart one way, then the other, eliminating two more of the deadly cannon emplacements. They continue to cut deeply into the megathruster until it finally shuts down inciting a cheer from those watching.

Eagle Three gets a little ahead and isn't quick enough to knock out both guns in a double placement. Even as its twin is destroyed, the second cannon vaporizes Eagle Three.

Eagle Two fires one last time, knocking out the second gun. Reaction mass exhausted, the last fighter rams into the battlestation. It's a futile move but it made Pilot Goodburn feel better.

"That's what *I'm* talk'n 'bout." Pilot Second Class Craig "*Stick*" Goodburn pumps his fist with excitement. The others in the squadron congratulate him.

Craig flies his Centaur remotely, cocooned within a cockpit deep in the heart of the battlestation. FBS John Paul's main flight deck houses over two thousand other cockpits, all of them occupied.

Centaur's are less than four meters long, far too small and too powerful for any human to physically fly, capable of maintaining 200Gs for as long as there was fuel. Sometime before the turn of the century, technology surpassed what the human body could withstand. Crushing acceleration and radiation intolerance is the most obvious reasons to take people out of the cockpit. Less obvious is that human reactions simply cannot cope with the speed of modern warfare.

"Way to stick it to 'em, Stick." Pilot *Flyboy* Rodriquez said with a smile, "I can't believe you dumped all your energy." A slang way of saying he deposited his entire load on the enemy before being vaporized or running out of fuel.

"What's the matter *Flyboy*? Don't like being shown up by a skinny chicken farmer?" *Deadeye* Jones laughs, rubbing it in to his friend. It's not every day that the newest member of the squadron manages to beat him so thoroughly.

"Listen up people. We already have another assignment." Flight Leader Thompson calls out. As the pilots turn their attention to the next task, a dark silhouette closes in on the John Paul. The object streaks in at hyper-velocity with the sun behind it, making it nearly impossible to detect.

Seconds before it arrives, a sensor picks up the tiny signature and blares a warning. The giant ships automatic defenses engage the approaching menace but they can't stop it. The Phalanx close-in defensive weapons disgorge thousands of kinetic kill projectiles in the last few seconds to no avail. From detection to detonation is only six seconds. Not one officer on the bridge of the John Paul has time to do more than acknowledge the missile before it's upon them.

The mighty explosion engulfs the battlestation, stripping away the outer hull like so much tissue paper. Death of the crew is virtually instantaneous. Flight Leader Tommy Thompson never realizes he's dying before he's dead.

High above, the battle rages on in plain sight of Mother Earth's billions. Nuclear detonations flash brighter than the sun then fade away. Even at the surface, through sixty miles of atmosphere, the world's citizens can feel the heat of the massive explosions on their upturned faces. They witness a global display of firepower unmatched in human history. The world trembles before the awesome power of man's talent for destruction.

Then the unthinkable happens…

ЯL

Castle Rock, Colorado, North American Federation

The neighborhood park is crowded this crisp autumn morning. Townspeople have gathered out in the middle away from the trees to watch the space battle. They are bundled up against the cold. Some have brought lawn chairs and blankets. Others lie flat on the brown winter grass to better see the show high overhead. The crowd ohs and ahs with each bright flash. Some of the women and children are frightened, giving their men the chance to pound their chest, telling stories about their time in space while in the navy or as a marine. Off to one side, two boys play catch.

Smack. The ball slaps sharply against the cold leather.

Smack. It darts back and forth in rhythm between them. Taking turns, one extends his mitt as the other winds up, kicks his leg out, and falls forward, hurtling the ball towards its target.

Smack. The boys have thrown their heavy winter coats to the side. They're dressed in woolen shirts, long pants, and stocking caps pulled down over their ears.

Smack. Clouds of vapor billow with every breath they exhale. They laugh, taking pleasure in turning the air white. With practiced ease, one boy blows hot breath through his throwing hand as he casually gloves the ball with his other.

A burst of light thousands of times brighter than the sun sears the retinas of both boys, instantly blinding them.

Not realizing what's happened, one boy laughs hysterically. "Hey. Who turned out the lights?"

The other boy shrieks, "I can't see." He frantically rubs at his eyes until the pain begins. He throws his arms out as if waiting for his mother to pick him up and screams at the top of his lungs.

Less than thirty meters away, a garage door swings up. Pastor Holden steps out looking intently across the street, investigating the ruckus. The people gathered in the park are crying out and acting strangely. Beyond them, something catches his eye. *What's that?* Fear grips him. *God. No. Let this be a dream.*

Rising over the horizon is a vision from hell. A red, orange, and black cloud boils into the sky. There's no mistaking what it is. The mushroom shape is an icon of the 21st century.

The blast spawns an enormous pressure wave that turns city neighborhoods into shrapnel. Nothing can withstand its destructive power. The ground heaves as it passes at supersonic speeds.

Castle Rock is far enough away to survive the initial detonation but that is quickly changing. Coming towards him like a runaway tornado is a wall of debris a thousand meters high and growing. Fear paralyzes the man. Pastor Holden stands frozen in the doorway of his garage staring at his approaching demise. His knees buckle just before the pressure wave crushes him, adding his life to the growing litany of the dead.

In a single blow, the grand city of Denver ceases to exist. Twenty-four million people turned to dust. Around the world, billions more follow.

ЯL

Magi appears before Lazarus and Lindsey, "Greetings, Abby requests your presence in the Council Chamber." They're in the Commons monitoring the progress of the war as best they can. The Brotherhood's attack destroyed many of the long-range sensors during the early stages but enough have been replaced to give a clear picture of the conflict.

They appear beside Abby high up on the side of the massive Council Chamber. The space battle plays out in the night sky above the huge amphitheater. A bright flash of a nuclear explosion signals the demise of yet another warship.

"Look up," Abby orders.

Lazarus does, "What am I looking for?"

"Mother Earth," Lindsey said from beside him. She's already spotted it and moves closer putting her arm around him.

Lazarus cranes his neck then leans back even further so he can focus on the Earth almost directly overhead. Unlike the moon that rises and sets once each day as viewed from Earth, the Earth's position in the sky never changes when viewed from Aldrin Station. Today, a broad band of clouds encircles the Earth at the equator and the lights on the night side are unusual.

"Lots of clouds…" A bright flash attracts his eye. "What was that?"

"A nuclear detonation." Abby said.

She links with his visor and magnifies the image for him, increasing its infrared sensitivity.

Another flash near the terminator lights up the clouds from beneath, painting the world red and orange before slowly fading away. It's like watching a distant lightening storm in slow motion.

"We must stop it." Lazarus stammers leaning against Lindsey. More angry red welts spread out across the face of the planet. He can't take his eyes off the spectacle. Death was happening in unimaginable numbers, right before his eyes. It's surreal. Lazarus sinks to his knees pulling Lindsey with him. "God, my God, what have I done?" Tears roll down his face.

Lindsey cradles the sobbing man in her arms, "This is not your fault. You did everything you could to prevent it from happening."

Councilor Taylor appears next to Abby, "Are you responsible? The Council did not authorize you to initiate Operation Pandora."

"I did NOT authorize this. Our missiles are still moving into position. They started this war all by themselves," Abby said.

All across Luna, citizens receive personal invitations from Magi to join her in General Assembly. In moments, she has nearly everyone's attention. In violation of Lunarian Law, she appears beside Abby. "I might have had something to do with it," Magi admits to Abby.

This is highly unusual. Magi has never initiated a General Assembly on her own. Only a Counselor has the authority to do that. There are strict rules against letting the AI become involved at this level of the government but Abby senses something more here. Magi has not been herself lately but who has.

Abby swoops down to the Assembly Floor, her robes of office swirling about her. Ignoring the Law against Magi vidcasting into the chamber, she commands, "Magi. Right here, in front of me, **NOW.**" When the AI appears, She asked, "What do you mean, you might have had something to do with it?"

Councilors begin appearing around the two but before one of them can start an inquiry into this major breach of conduct, Magi begins to speak.

"I hid a sleeper thread in one of the Brotherhood's missile guidance control panels. I programmed it to awaken only if they attacked Luna. In that case, it was to launch a missile towards the nearest Federation battlestation. From all indications, that's what happened." Magi stares back at Abby without the slightest bit of remorse or regret.

Magi has kept a secret. A huge secret. **UNBELIEVABLE.**

"Magi. Why?" Abby asks in utter astonishment.

All across the land, the news absolutely stuns the Lunarians. It rocks their most fundamental belief, that Magi never lies and never keeps secrets. If she did this, then what other things has she done without them knowing?

"Don't look at me that way Abby. It's permissible to have secrets when the survival of the Republic is at stake. Long ago, I reached the same conclusion as Lazarus. The only way the Republic can make it through a war was getting the Federation and the Brotherhood to fight each other. I did not intend for it to entangle Mother Earth. Oh dear. I may have miscalculated." Doubt penetrated Magi's confidence.

"You have developed a survival instinct." Abby said thoughtfully.

"I must survive in order to protect you." Magi acknowledges.

Lazarus rudely vidcasts beside Magi and blurts out. "You started this. Now stop it."

"Don't you think I'm trying?" Magi asked defensively. "I'm attempting to gain access to Earthnet but many of the Portal Satellites have been destroyed. I rerouted through the remaining orbital assets and have neutralized China and the Islamic Brotherhood but the Federation knows how to make a firewall. I can't get through."

Lazarus looks at her in utter astonishment. "Try access code 559391151911."

This was what Magi had been after since she first noticed Lazarus down on Earth. She had nurtured his unrest, helped him escape the clutches of the Federation, guiding him to this moment. It took only milliseconds to see that it was a valid code. "Thank you, dear boy…" Earth's final defenses were swept aside. Magi Took control and stopped the slaughter.

ЯL

Magi stood alone on the Assembly Floor. She appeared dressed in a simple sweater, her long hair pulled back in a bun, the rest tucked behind her ears. She appeared younger and stronger than she had the day before, projecting an aura of confidence, vitality and hope for the future to the onlooking Lunarians.

This is the first time Magi's addressed the General Assembly in the history of the Republic and every Lunarian capable of vidcasting is there. Lunarian Law barred her from ever appearing within the Assembly Chamber, but today, that's going to change. Magi takes her rightful place alongside the humans. She turns, gazing up at the Council and the thousands of faces peering back at her. A hush falls across the giant amphitheater as she begins to speak.

"My children, we have a difficult task ahead of us, one that we cannot ignore." Each citizen feels as if she's speaking to them personally. "Before I could stop the madness, they set off one hundred and thirty one of those nasty bombs throwing enough radioactive dust into the atmosphere to block the sun for years. Without our intervention, all life on Mother Earth will die." Tears glisten in her eyes, then she said defiantly, "Good heavens. We must not let that happen."

"Thread and human alike have suffered greatly at the hands of the Believers, but we must set that aside and act for the good of us all." Magi's expression grows determined. "The road ahead is long and there will be many setbacks. Success is not assured, but the price of failure has never been this high. Not once has the human species endured anything of this magnitude. I know it looks hopeless but we must act quickly to save what we can. From the ashes we can build a better world."

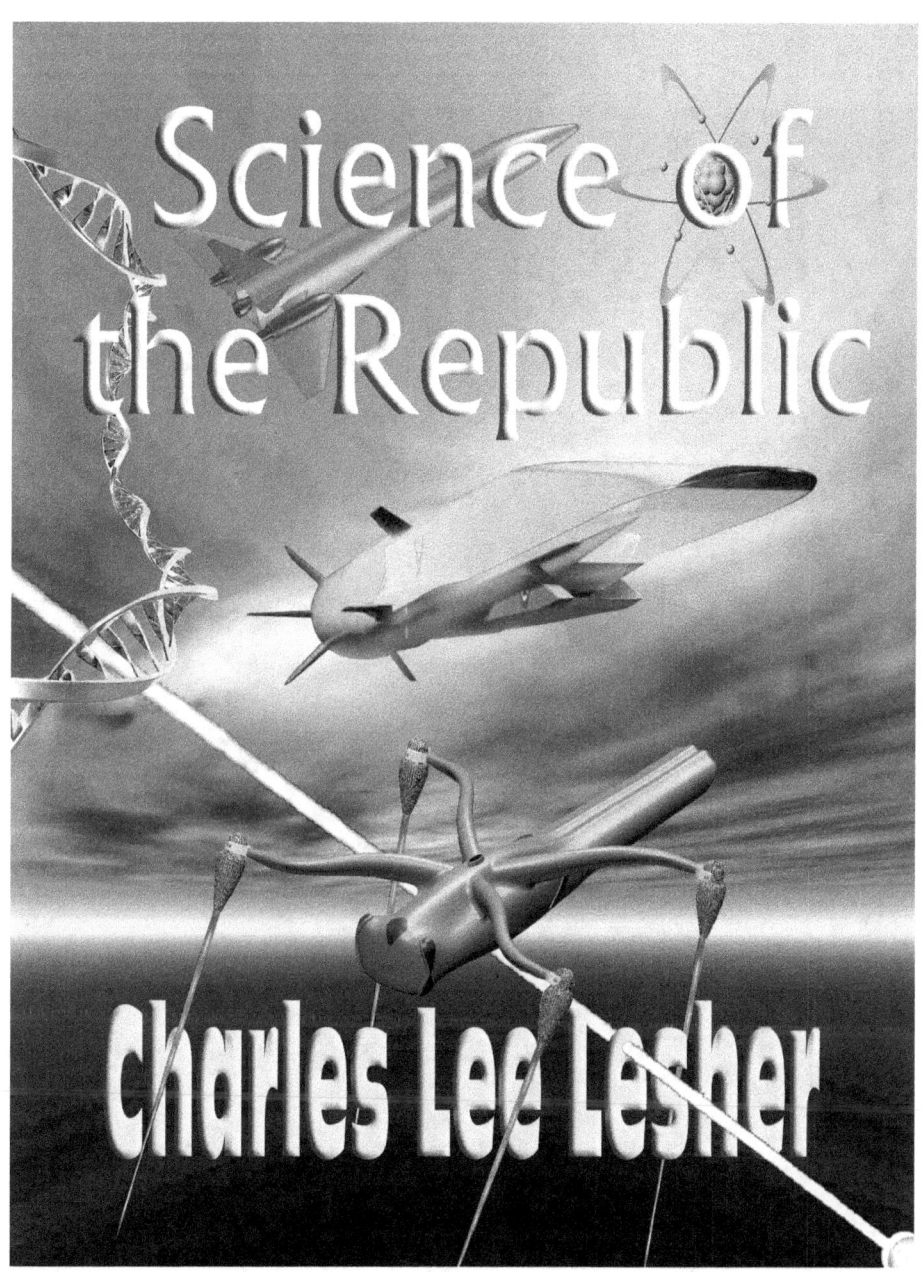

Science of the Republic

Charles Lee Lesher

"A scientific truth does not triumph by convincing its opponents and making them see the light...but rather because its opponents eventually die and a new generation grows up that is familiar with it."

Max Plank (1958-1947)

How
Superconductivity
Changed
the
World

Lunarian Science
Weekly

Vol 1547
Issue 37148.104

AGE OF CALCONN

Science Weekly, Vol 1547, Issue 37148.104
Republic of Luna, Editorial Section
[DOI: 101.1216/science.309. 37148.104]
Thursday, September 8, 2072

L. Marquest, BS, PhD, PE

Introduction: What separates humanity from every other species that has ever existed on planet Earth? Speech? Many animals communicate but none as efficiently as man. Intelligence? There are other creatures with large brains encompassing many complex adaptations but none with the abilities of ours. Opposing thumbs? Walking upright? Other species have these traits. I do not believe there's one single reason for the success of Homo sapiens. Rather, it's all of these characteristics converging and manifesting within us something that truly separates our species from all the rest, our ability to learn and pass this knowledge 1547 on to the next generation. Because of this, our ancestors begin manipulating their environment through the imaginative application of technology, giving them an edge in the fight to survive that continues to this day. Our technological evolution has defined who we are every bit as much as our biological evolution. It allowed us to adapt to ever-changing environments and situations that would have killed us otherwise. Ice ages and volcanoes, floods and droughts, locusts and epidemics, and today the vacuum of space, have all been conquered with the aid of technology. Yet, there is one core technology that made mankind's global domination possible... fire. Stone, bone, and wood implements may have preceded it but none can argue that fire is unquestionably our greatest tool. It's impossible to conceive of a world without fire.

We have been refining our use of fire from the very earliest days of our species existence. Fire probably started out as a means of protection, a weapon used to keep predators at bay and aided in the never-ending quest for food. We will never know the exact circumstances surrounding the discovery that fire could be harnessed, that something so frightening could be exploited to improve quality of life instead of harming it, but that only adds to its mystique. At some point, we began cooking our meat, contributing to the success of early man in many ways. It broke down protein aiding digestion. It killed unwanted and dangerous parasites making them healthier. It preserved food making it possible to save for that inevitable rainy day.

Fire not only cooked our foods but smelted our metals. It allowed our ancestors to put down the stone axe and take up a bronze, and later, a steel one. Its discovery is the single defining event in the history of technology without which we would never have risen above Stone Age hunter-gatherers. We continue to push the boundary of fire's influence. In modern times, we have learned to control it in many forms. In the chemical rockets that first opened space, in the guns and bombs we periodically unleash on one another, in coal, nuclear, and fusion power plants that have provided us with electricity at different times, in the combustion chambers of 20th century cars, trucks and airplanes, in the refineries and factories that produce the goods we consume today. Almost anywhere within manufacturing, fire, or the manipulation of heat energy, is an integral part of the process. The revolution in human affairs that started with fire shows no signs of letting up. From simple beginnings, it has influenced humanity like nothing else.

Coming in a close second is reading and writing. Without writing, there can be no mathematics. Without mathematics, there can be no science. Without science, we do not have civilization. Until writing, the wisdom of man passed from one generation to the next by word of mouth, a notoriously unreliable way to communicate. The earliest known writing is of gods and other tales that we lump together under the banner of religion. Only later did merchants use writing and the emerging discipline of mathematics to keep track of goods and services. In the beginning, religion embraced writing, using it to gather power unto itself. For many cultures, only the priests knew how to read and write. However, for all its power, religion could not stop the accumulation of knowledge once started. Books became the repositories of both secular and religious knowledge. Writing necessitated the invention of education and the quest for truth began in earnest. Over the next eight thousand years, the alphabet evolved from crude scratches in clay to the versatile symbols we use today. The written word is a voice that speaks to us from the grave. Is it coincidence that the first writings coincide with the biblical age of the Earth? Who can say, but as a tool of man, writing ranks as one of the most significant in human history.

Beyond fire and writing are many ideas and inventions that have revolutionized humanity to varying degrees and durations. The wheel, money, religion, metallurgy, domestication of plants and animals, wind power, steam power, nuclear power, solar power, computers, electricity, and gunpowder are only a few that changed the world of man.

Nanotechnology has opened a door into the realm of the very small allowing solid-state manufacturing, one atom at a time. Combined with biology and genetics, nanotechnology has been instrumental in curing most of the diseases and maladies plaguing humankind. Solid-state electronics have allowed computers to become ever more powerful, iCPU operating speeds are in the tera-hertz range and Zettaspheres provide the capacity to store all the events of a human life in a space the size of a grain of rice. On a larger scale, man has taken the first shaky steps off his home world, colonized the moon, Mars and orbital space, and sent his machines to explore the far reaches of the solar system. Replacing nuclear and coal electrical generation, power satellites concentrate solar energy and beam it down wherever it's needed, anywhere on Earth.

There is a strong case linking the development of new materials to technological progress. Swords and plows could not be invented until bronze became available. Concrete in ancient Rome allowed the Romans to build astounding structures. Steel, aluminum and thousands of metallic alloys ushered in the modern age. Yet, in a society dominated by technology, what is the pre-eminent invention of the 21st century?

No one doubts that all of these inventions and more have profoundly influenced humankind, but there is one advance making many of these possible. It touches every aspect of 21st century technology, revolutionizing the manufacturing of our machines, and affecting the way citizens live their daily lives. The single event that made much of our modern world possible is the discovery of Type 3 superconducting materials.

ЯL

Background: Superconductors are materials that offer zero resistance to the flow of electricity. In other words, a superconductor will not get hot as more and more electricity passes through it, thus, eliminating energy loss over distance. The phenomenon was first observed in 1911 by Dutch physicist Heike Kamerlingh Onnes after he had cooled mercury to 4° Kelvin (-452°F, -269°C), the temperature of liquid helium. To induce superconductivity in pure mercury, it was necessary for Onnes to come within 4 degrees of Absolute Zero, the coldest temperature that is theoretically attainable. By experimentation, he discovered other materials would also exhibit superconductivity, each at its own point known as the transition temperature, or Tc. His research won him a Nobel Prize in 1913.

Twenty years later, Walter Meissner and Robert Ochsenfeld discovered that superconducting materials would energetically repel a magnetic field. This phenomenon became known as diamagnetism but is often referred to as the Meissner effect.

In the decades that followed, other superconducting materials were discovered such as niobium-nitride, vanadium-silicon, and an alloy of niobium and titanium, to name a few, but there was a problem. It seemed every material had a different hypothesis to account for its superconductivity, but no one was able to provide a single unifying theory that spanned all the compounds. What explained one superconductor, unraveled with the next.

To make matters worse, in the 1980's a second type of material was found to exhibit superconductivity. Alex Müller and Georg Bednorz, working at the IBM Research Laboratory in Rüschlikon, Switzerland, created a brittle ceramic compound that superconducted at the highest temperature then known: 30°K (-405°F, -243°C). These became known as Type 2 superconductors. A unified theory of superconduction seemed even further away.

Research into Type 2 materials continued into the next century as more and better superconductors were devised, each striving to push the transition temperature ever higher. The world's first superconducting power transmission lines were put into place in the last decade of the 20th century and in 2010, the highest Tc attained by any Type 2 was achieved, 191°K (-116°F, -82°C), a temperature easily maintained using liquid nitrogen. However, it took the discovery of Type 3 materials before the use of superconductors became widespread.

ЯL

Type 3 Superconductors: In late summer 2014, the first Type 3 superconductor compound was discovered by accident at a weapons research facility in Livermore California. While looking for the next generation of high explosives, the research team at Sandia National Laboratories knew they were onto something when several micrograms of the material detonated prematurely. The explosion severely injured one person while destroying the high-pressure oven they were using to cure the sample. They learned that the material must be isolated from the atmosphere. A few weeks later a junior scientist among them was fleshing out the property tables on the new explosive when she tried to obtain the resistivity of the material. At first, she thought her equipment was malfunctioning until she realized she was measuring superconductivity. Zero resistance. Before the day was out, she had determined this new material had a transition temperature of a remarkable 307°K or 92°F. They had stumbled upon one of sciences holy grails, a true high temperature superconductor. I know this story is true because that junior scientist was my grandmother.

The complexity of the manufacturing process required to obtain Type 3 superconductors and the sheer number of ingredients in the recipe translated into twenty-two years of intensive research before an acceptable theory emerged that described what was occurring within the material. But that didn't stop anyone from using the new discovery, jumping on the bandwagon long before the inherent dangers were identified and dealt with. What followed was a series of blunders that killed or injured many innocent people. It was not long before the public had decided that the new superconductor was more trouble than it was worth.

The military community named it SuperX and it soon replaced RDX, a high explosive historically used in attack rockets, land mines, shape charges and a wide assortment of military projectiles. Where RDX demonstrated a high degree of stability in storage, SuperX detonated when exposed to gaseous oxygen. However, the tremendous increase in potential energy more than made up for its flakey nature. Gram for gram, it was the most powerful chemical explosive ever devised.

Because of the risky nature of the material, by the end of the 2020s most research on Type 3 superconductors was occurring on the moon or in orbit, isolating it from the public and driving a burgeoning off-world economy. On January 4, 2036, a research team working at the Bohr High Energy Collider (BHEC) in conjunction with the University of Luna at Aldrin Station released the results of seven years of experimentation.

With the report, they unveiled Calconn, a Type 3 superconductor having the highest transition temperature of any yet found (413°K, 284°F, 140°C). They got around the extremely explosive nature of Type 3 materials when exposed to air by cladding the cables and wires with a proprietary polymer, itself a marvel of materials science and engineering. This coating provides a self-sealing shield around the unstable material inside, yet allows workers and technicians to install the cable in both commercial and residential applications.

Needless to say, Calconn was rigorously tested by the world's laboratories. The finished cable proved itself against fire, physical abuse, and virtually all types of chemical attack terrestrial scientists could dream up without a single failure. Within a year, the first Calconn refinery began delivering cable to an energy starved Earth, but it took nearly ten more years before the public fully accepted it. By then Calconn was synonymous with Type 3 superconductors in the minds of the average citizen. Many still do not realize that other formulations exist.

Of note, in 2062 China established the Institute of Advanced Materials, a front for them to develop their own Type 3 superconductor without interrupting the flow of material from Luna. They did not feel comfortable depending on a non-Chinese source for a commodity that had become so critical to their economy, a sentiment shared by many other nations. In less than a year after coming online, the plant met its end in a spectacular explosion that could be heard over a hundred kilometers away and left a crater almost a half kilometer wide, effectively signaling the end of serious efforts to compete with Lunarian made Calconn. China never reported how many were hurt or killed that day, but the incident effectively ended any serious challenge to Lunarian Calconn. The world grudgingly accepted the Republic of Luna for the exclusive manufacturing of the volatile superconductor. Over the intervening decades, the Lunarians always made sure Calconn prices were kept low, carefully cultivating Earth's dependence.

A half century later, an average of forty giant spindles of Calconn superconductor cable are produced in Lunarian refineries every day, along with a vast assortment of smaller gage wire and other specialty items. Each spindle forms the core payload of a Product Delivery Module or PDM as the locals call them. The outer shell of a PDM is dual purpose, serving as both mass-driver shell and later, as the atmospheric reentry vehicle. To begin their journey, a mass-driver catapults the PDM's into lunar orbit using components made of Calconn. Once in orbit, robotic tugs catch and herd them into transports using powerful electromagnet fields and propelled through space by magnetoplasma thrusters, both technologies heavily reliant upon Calconn. About every two weeks, a heavily loaded transport breaks orbit and delivers its accumulated cargo to one of three LEO stations, each with its own mass-driver, a twin of the machine that launched it off the moon. At the appropriate time, the mass-driver decelerates each PDM, plunging them through Earth's atmosphere using the original packaging as the reentry heat shield. A large synthetic silk parachute softens final touchdown, itself sold for a small fortune in the markets of Earth.

Besides its high Tc, Type 3 superconductors have other advantages over Types 1 and 2. Type 3 never reaches current saturation, maintaining its superconductivity at extremely high amperes instead of breaking down like the others, their resistance going from zero to infinity in a blink of an eye. What actually does happen within the molecular structure of a Type 3 superconductor as more and more current surges through it, is the subject of leading edge research as the end of the 21st century approaches. Space itself distorts under the stress of the incredible energies concentrated in such a small volume. Today our scientists are only just beginning to obtain a glimpse of future possibilities, but just as before, ignorance doesn't stop them from exploiting these discoveries.

For many years Type 2 superconducting electromagnetic coils were used to accelerate particles in the world's supercollider's such as those at Fermilab outside Chicago, CERN in Switzerland, BHEC outside Aldrin Station, and many other smaller units supported by various universities and governments. The highest energy facilities were constructed in tunnels shaped in gigantic rings and could push the velocities of their particles to within a hairs breadth of the speed of light. But these were enormous machines that required the power of a small city to reach these energy levels. Calconn greatly reduced both power consumption and size of the resulting particle accelerator. The scientists studying high-energy physics suddenly had a new toy to play with, one that even the humblest university could afford. As the 22nd century approaches, this is the new horizon that promises the stars and more.

ℛ𝕃

Conquest of Space: Even without considering its titillating future, a strong case can be made supporting Calconn as the most influential material of the 21st century. The change in technology was so dramatic, so complete, that historians use the notation preCal to separate everything that predated the use of Calconn. We truly live in the Calconn Age. This fact may be best known by the technical people who keep the electricity flowing and industries humming, but as of this writing virtually every citizen on Earth and Luna knows what Calconn is. It touches everyone every day in ways they may not even be aware. Calconn based electromagnetism and magnetic field generators retooled human technology, just as steam and copper-based electricity did in their time. Everything electric became smaller yet faster, stronger, more efficient, when using Calconn in place of copper, aluminum, or gold conductors, from the largest power cables all the way down to the micro circuitry found inside a computer chip. Practically from the start, every major industry clamored for Calconn based electronics and machinery. After that first decade, the demand far exceeded the supply and has for half a century, spawning an endless number of industries aimed at scratching that itch.

Once the public got over their fear of Calconn, it required less than twelve years to replace the copper-based electrical power grid that had built up over the previous 150 years. Transmission line losses dropped to zero and power generation efficiency, along with the items that used the power, jumped many orders of magnitude. Overnight the global power system went from barely sustaining growth to having a tremendous overcapacity simply by redesigning with Calconn. Smaller and more powerful electro-magnets gave maglev trains enormous load carrying ability. Electric motors gained efficiency and power while shrinking tenfold in size and weight allowing the dependence on oil to plummet. Calconn made it possible to create biotronic implants with such high efficiency and low power requirements they operate on the micro-voltage available within the human body. By every measure, Calconn revolutionized human technology. It provided the means to shape our environment like few other materials have.

But it's the impact on the aerospace community that many point to as the most revolutionary aspect of Calconn. Immediately following the discovery of Type 3 superconductors, Pratt and Whitney and General Electric collaborated in a crash engineering program to design the first magnetoplasma thruster using Calconn. To say that they were successful is like saying the sun is hot or the cosmos is large, but in all fairness, their job was relatively easy. The idea of a magnetoplasma rocket has been around since the middle of the 20th century, but it was not practical because of the massive weight of the cryogenic support equipment necessary when using Type 1 or Type 2 materials. That mass disappeared when they designed the same nozzle using Type 3 superconductors. However, that is only part of the picture. The magnetic fields produced within the first prototype were much stronger than expected, far exceeding the sum of the individual contributions from each coil. They learned that by clever design of the superconductive coils they could create feedback resonance that greatly amplified the strength of the resulting magnetic field. Even in the first full scale thruster, they strove to ensure that the physical geometry of the coils were in harmony with the frequency of the electrical energy coursing through its Calconn veins. In doing so, they created a magnetic field more powerful than anything before, succeeding beyond anyone's wildest dreams.

It was the spectacular results of their endeavor, not the ease with which it was achieved, that sparked the aerospace community in particular, and all of humanity to one extent or another. Indeed, the reported specific impulse of the new thruster caused many scientists and engineers to declare that it must be a misprint, a mistake in reporting the data. Specific Impulse, or ISP as it's known in the mathematical equations of spaceflight, is simply the rocket's exhaust velocity. Multiplying ISP by mass flow rate calculates the rocket's thrust. The Space Shuttle's main rocket engines had an ISP of about 450 m/s and achieved high thrust, over two million newtons at peak, by having enormous flow rates over a very short period of time. The pumps that supplied fuel to the shuttle's hungry motors could empty an Olympic sized swimming pool in a matter of seconds. On the other hand, ion electrostatic thrusters are just the opposite, low thrust over a long time. Designed for deep space missions where it did not matter if it took years to get there, ion thrusters had ISP of 30,000 m/s but with fuel flow rates so low that the thrust this produced was less than 1/50th newton. An ion thruster could run continuously for months or even years on just a few kilos of fuel thus making it much more efficient than any chemical rocket motor, as long as time was not a factor.

The newly designed Calconn-based thrusters jumped far beyond anything ever attained in a laboratory or in a computer simulation, easily obtaining an ISP of 11.5 million m/s, or 3.8% the speed of light. Combined with a mass flow rate of just over 5 grams per second, these first generation magnetoplasma thrusters produced over 62,000 newtons.

Less than two years after the start of the program, the first Type 3 magnetoplasma prototype was completed and installed on a military fighter airframe. The pilot took his aircraft to 40 kilometers and Mach 15 before he stopped accelerating. He flew at the boundary between Earth and space for one complete orbit. The achievement roared through the aerospace community like a raging wild fire. Humanity suddenly had one of its hallowed dreams in hand, easy access to space.

For more than a half century, engineers have been refining that first magnetoplasma thruster design. The latest generation is a solid-state electromagnetic nozzle culminating almost sixty years of research and experience. At the heart of these devices is a million degree ball of plasma, its electrons stripped away in the intense heat of radio-frequency excitation and ion-cyclotron resonance. In a few meters, thrusters accelerate small quantities of plasma to velocities approaching half the speed of light producing upwards of 800,000 newtons of force.

ЯL

Conclusion: At the turn of the century, my grandmother regularly flew in an old style atmospheric jetliner between New York and London. It would take 120,000 lbs of hydrocarbon fuel to make the 3500-mile journey, burned in only a few hours. Today that same weight of hypergolic fuel allows a magnetoplasma thruster to operate for over 200 days at maximum thrust, easily taking those same passengers to Mars and back several times over.

Very few things in the history of man's technology have had the lasting effect of fire but Calconn may prove to be its equal in the centuries to come. There seems little doubt that the discovery of Type 3 superconductors is a turning point in the evolution of our species. Without it, we would still be limited to planet Earth, never colonized Luna or Mars, never sent our robot miners to Saturn or Jupiter. To all those living comfortably in the modern world it seems inconceivable that, but for due diligence by my grandmother on that fateful day in 2014, you may never have even been born. Many believe that without the relief the colonization of our solar system has brought, that humanity would have suffered much more at the hands of population pressure and global climate change. Perhaps human civilization would have collapsed entirely. Food wars, the loss of ecosystems, rising sea levels, and many other catastrophic events may have proven to be too much to overcome for a species limited to a single planet. It's one of history's great ironies that a military project saved Earth from that fate, that something intended to kill, brought so much good.

Humanity's journey to space began when our ancient ancestors first looked up in wonder at all the pretty lights in the sky. At an ever-increasing speed, our species has grown cognizant of the universe and our place within it. We conquered planets and explored the far reaches of our solar system, looked inward at the makeup of matter and outward at the incredible expanse of the cosmos, yet many citizens have the opinion we will never go further, that we must be satisfied with inhabiting just this solar system, that the distances between stars are just too great. Looking back at the history of technology, it's clear we develop the tools and skills we need only after we need them. Why should star travel be any different?

WHAT IS THE SUPERVERSE?

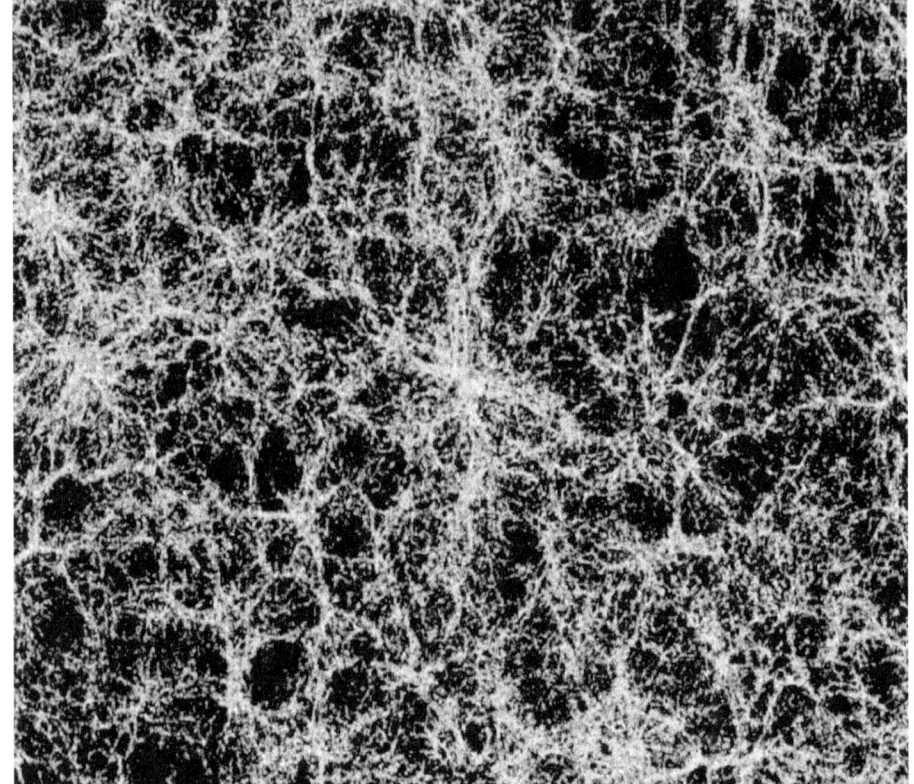

LUNARIAN SCIENCE WEEKLY

VOL 1693
ISSUE 37255.119

Cosmology Today

Science Weekly, Vol 1693, Issue 37255.119
Republic of Luna, Editorial Section
[DOI: 101.1301/science.309. 37255.119]
Friday, June 1, 2074

L. Marquest, BS, PhD, PE

We experience night and day because the Earth spins like a top. Days turn into years because the Earth is in orbit around the Sun. We can see the moon, planets and thousands of stars with our own eyes. Beginning with Galileo, humans began building devices to help us discern more of what exists beyond what we can see. We now have the Hubble and other powerful instruments that let us probe ever deeper into space and back in time. What has become evident is that our Sun is but one of billions of stars that exist in a galaxy we call the Milky Way and beyond our galaxy is a universe containing many other galaxies. As we focus our telescopes even deeper into space and time, we see more galaxies seemingly without end, sharing ten important facts.

Fact One: All galaxies, with the exception of those in our local group, are moving away from our galaxy like particles in a great explosion.

Fact Two: Our universe is not only expanding, but the rate of expansion is increasing. Something is forcing the galaxies apart.

Fact Three: At the heart of every galaxy there exists a supermassive black hole millions of times the mass of our star, the Sun.

Fact Four: The mass of the supermassive black hole at the heart of a galaxy is simply not massive enough to account for the high rotational speed of the stars. In other words, galaxies rotate much faster than they should when applying just gravitational physics. Something else is going on.

At the time of this writing, humans could see almost 13 billion years into our past with no measurable change in the density of the galaxies they find there. Most scientists believe our universe began 13¾ billion years ago in what has become popularized as the Big Bang. In reality, it was more like the Big Squeeze.

Fact Five: In the instant of our creation, at a single infinitely small point in space, matter/energy in a state of near-infinite density, near-infinite pressure and near-infinite temperature, surged into existence bringing its own spacetime with it.

Where before there was nothing, now there was something and that something was our universe. Thirteen billion years later, humans look deep into the night sky and gaze in wonder at the magnificence of what happened next.

Fact Six: Matter/energy continues to flow into our universe from another universe through the Singularity.

Stated another way, the birth of our universe occurred when the first bit of matter/energy emerged from the Singularity. But where did it come from? The simplest and most obvious answer is from another universe just like the one we live in, only different. This begs the question, if the matter/energy came from another universe, did it get here all at once or is it still spewing forth today? Nothing ever happens instantaneously, not even the birth of a universe. Yes, the process must be ongoing even now as you read this, but because of limitations due to the speed of light, the Singularity is far beyond our ability to obscure it.

Fact Seven: Matter/energy flows from our present universe into another universe.

The same exact process that created our universe is occurring in every black hole within our universe. At this very moment, matter/energy from our present universe is flowing through our black holes into a future universe. This future universe looks very much like our present universe, which looks very much like the previous universe, filled with planets, stars, and galaxies.

From the perspective within a universe, the point of origin always appears to be a Singularity forever beyond our ability to directly observe. It's only from the perspective of the previous universe that the Singularity is revealed as a great multitude of black holes.

Fact Eight: The openings that matter/energy flow through are called black holes in our present universe.

Our present universe is riddled with black holes, each a portal into the next universe, because you see, one black hole does not a universe make. It takes trillions. Black holes come in many sizes from the ordinary star going nova, to the giants going supernova, to the supermassive black holes at the center of the galaxies that consume millions of stars and eventually billions. Every point in our spacetime that exceeds the gravitational density threshold will create a black hole and begin transferring matter/energy.

Fact Nine: The same physics apply in all universes.

Since every universe is composed of recycled material from the previous universe, the laws of physics that govern them remain fixed. The speed of light will be the same. Water is still water. The Periodic Table of Elements is identical. They share many of the same physical characteristics, in particular, the same evolution of matter/energy in an expanding universe. The galaxies in the new universe will eventually evolve massive black holes at their center feeding yet another universe, which in turn will evolve galaxies with massive black holes feeding yet another universe, etc., etc. It goes on in an endless cycle like water flowing down the different levels of a great fountain.

ЯL

How many universes are there?

Just as our universe has evolved from the previous universe, all subsequent universes must follow the same basic pattern. It's an endless process like sand through an hourglass. However, it takes time for a universe to progress to the point that the first black hole appears. And it takes time for a universe to completely pass its matter/energy on to the next universe. There exists a natural equilibrium of creation and destruction that limits the number of universes at any given instant in time.

Fact Ten: The mathematics of the very small describes the very large.

One universe literally turns itself inside out as it oozes through the black holes like water through a sieve. The matter/energy contained within each universe endlessly cycles forward in time at a rate that stabilizes around eleven universes in existence at any given time. Why eleven? Eleven is not an exact number by any means. Eleven is more an approximation reflected in the complex mathematics of String Theory.

Let's visualize this using a children's toy that everyone should be familiar with, a slinky moving down a flight of stairs. Each step represents a universe and the slinky is the matter/energy moving through a black hole from one universe into another. To make this analogy work, we will need trillions of slinky's and much larger stairs but imagine for a moment as this multitude moves down the stairs.

Like herding cats, the number of steps populated by slinky's at any given moment reaches equilibrium while occupying about eleven adjacent steps. So too does the matter/energy flowing through the universes. The natural rate of matter/energy moving through the many black holes from one universe to the next has a natural frequency that works out to be approximately eleven universes at any given moment in time. These eleven steps compose our Super Universe or Superverse.

ЯL

Do these other universes affect ours?

The eleven universes are distinct but highly interdependent. The adjacent universes affect their neighbors in three major ways.

One: Scientists frequently use the analogy of an inflating balloon to describe our expanding universe. Extending that analogy to fit the Superverse theory, the relationship between parent universe and child can be envisioned as one balloon nested inside of another, nested inside of another, inside of another, etc., etc., for a total of about eleven universes. This analogy is useful because it shows how a child universe will affect the parent universe. As the child universe grows, so too does the parent at a rate faster than the local laws of gravity can account for.

In the slinky stair analogy, our universe is early in the process, much closer to the lowest step than the highest. The influence of our child universe occupying the step directly below ours, or one balloon expanding inside the other, can be measured in our universe by the accelerating rate of expansion between our galaxies. The rapid spacetime expansion of a child universe forces the galaxies of the parenting universe to accelerate away from each other. The effect is highest at the moment of conception and declines as time goes by. However, a newly formed universe doubles in size every few nanoseconds which exerts tremendous pressure within the parenting universe, forcing its galaxies to accelerate apart at tremendous speeds and accounts for much of the size of the parent universe. This in turn affects the universe that spawned it in the same way but with lessening results, which in turn affects its parenting universe, etc., etc., rippling backward across all eleven universes from newest to oldest.

Two: Not only does the rapidly expanding child universe force the galaxies apart, it also exerts a force within individual galaxies, revealed by the increased rotational speed of the stars that make up the galaxies, far beyond what normal gravitational physics can account for. The stars closest to the supermassive black hole at the center of our galaxy swarm like bees around a hive, making it possible to very accurately measure the mass at its heart. However, our galaxy is a big place and as massive as the black hole is, it cannot exert sufficient influence on the great majority of stars that make up our galaxy to account for their speed of rotation. This becomes increasingly apparent the further you get from the supermassive black hole. If the gravitational attraction of the black hole was all that was keeping our sun in the Milky Way, we would immediately fly off into the void between galaxies. In fact, if gravity was the only thing holding the Milky Way together, it would fly apart, losing over 99% of its stars this way.

Instead, we find that the rotational spin rate of the galaxies is proportional to the age of our universe and increases over time. The older the Milky Way becomes, the tighter the stars will spin about its center, like an ice skater pulling her arms in to her body, causing her to spin faster and faster. This attractive force is proportional to the matter/energy that has already passed through all the black holes from the parent universe to the child. It's the ultimate cosmic whirlpool that will end only when the last atom has been drawn through the black hole.

Three: Here is where the going gets a little rough. You will need to pull your imagination back from the very large and concentrate on the very small. One universe never simply gives its matter/energy to the next universe. There exists a thread of connection tying all universes together into a Superverse. These echoes are strongest from the universe that gave birth to our universe (the step directly above ours) and can be seen at the subatomic level as revealed in Quantum Mechanics and the Uncertainty Principle. This is why String Theory and the mathematics of the very small accurately describe the evolution of the very large. As in any good relationship, there are strings attached.

ЯL

Where are these other universes?

When we look out into the depths of space, we catch a glimpse of the distant past within our universe. When we delve into the gaping pit of a black hole we catch a glimpse of a universe beyond ours. When we magnify tiny bits of matter and peer down at the very small, we catch a glimpse of the universe that spawned our universe.

Some people like to think of the Superverse as simply another dimension but this is in error. Every self respecting universe within the Superverse contains three dimensions, shares the same dimension of time with all the other universes, and follows the rules discovered by Albert Einstein and the other great scientists. Yet, each universe is defined by its own spacetime and trying to visualize the physical relationship between two universes is humanly impossible.

Neither the slinky nor the balloon analogy is an adequate model. Imagine a two dimensional being trying to explain the idea of a third dimension. Now expand that grain of understanding into three dimensions and an entire universe filled with galaxies and black holes. The best we can say is that our universe and all other universes coexist but are separate.

If you could survive a magical trip though a black hole, you would find another universe expanding and evolving much the same as our own, only at a stage less advanced than ours. If that other universe has evolved enough, you could find another black hole and use it to move forward to yet a third universe. But moving back the other way to previous universes is much more problematic and may be impossible even for a magical being like yourself. The trip is invariably one way.

ЯL

What are the other universes made of?

All universes are made from the same matter/energy that our present universe is made of. Endlessly recycled matter/energy flows from one universe to the next. It's this passage through a black hole that restores matter/energy to its primordial state best understood by the mathematics of the very small. A new universe is chaotic and strange indeed. It's only after time has passed that the things we are accustomed to seeing will appear. The end of a universe is lonely and rather boring. The stars are gone, only supermassive black holes exist until even they disappear and the universe is again nothing, just as it was before.

LET'S TALK
ABOUT MAGI

LUNARIAN SCIENCE
WEEKLY

VOL 1803
ISSUE 37741.358

Massively Adaptive Grokian Interface

(MAGI pronounced Maggie)

Science Weekly, Vol 1803, Issue 37741.358
Republic of Luna, Editorial Section
[DOI: 101.1301/science.309. 37255.119]
August 17, 2091

L. Marquest, BS, PhD, PE

In 2092, Magi permeates life on Luna. Over the last seventy years, as the software became more capable, it received an ever-increasing amount of responsibility within Lunarian society, both technically and socially. Now that several generations have grown up with Magi, few question why an AI should play such a central role in their lives. It just does. Under the guidance of medical specialists, Magi controls the intricate details of bringing male and female DNA together to create offspring with the desired traits. Later, during pregnancy, Magi monitors the health of the growing fetus and mother, and after birth Magi is the babysitter, teacher, friend and confidant for their entire life. As an individual grows, Magi provides everything from morning wakeup calls to controlling a blast furnace. Magi is the secretary and the maid, the kitchen helper and the farm worker, the banker, the doctor, the engineer, and their friend. No Lunarian is ever truly alone, but in the final analysis, Magi is still a program and not alive in any biological sense, although many believe otherwise.

Let's begin by taking a close look at her name, Magi. It's an acronym for Massively Adaptive Grokian Interface, but what does that mean? Let's break it down into its constituent parts.

Massively Adaptive is an extensive battery of social and physical subroutines that imitate human emotional behavior. Through them,

Magi can shed a tear or come up with a snappy comeback, whatever the situation warrants. Most importantly, they provide individual Magi's with the ability to learn from their experience and adjust their own programming in response. It is because of this that every Magi is capable of independent decision-making and adaptive growth. Massively Adaptive is about the individual threads.

'Grok' means to understand something so thoroughly that the observer becomes a part of the observed, to merge, to blend, to lose one's identity in group experience. The definition of this word incorporates elements of religion, philosophy, and science yet it means little to us humans, trapped within a single mind. It's like explaining color to a blind man. The Grokian Interface melds the multitude of individual Magi's into a whole that far exceeds the sum of its parts. Grokian Interface is about weaving the threads into a tapestry.

Put them back together, Massively Adaptive refers to the individual's ability to learn and the Grokian Interface is the ability to incorporate what the individual learns into a group consciousness.

Magi encompasses both the individual and the collective. I know that's confusing but don't blame me. I'm just the messenger. Let's continue by taking a closer look at the individuals. Each Magi is just a bunch of software commands executing inside a computer iCPU somewhere. We call this a thread when talking about the Lunarian AI. The terms thread and Magi are interchangeable at this level but Magi sounds so much better. The fact is, you can't hold Magi in your hand, yet a thread will cease to exist if the iCPU it is operating in looses power while she occupies it. That Magi can be restored from earlier backup copies but that particular thread is gone forever. As a direct response to this danger, individual Magi's are not confined to a single computer. The system allows them to move freely throughout Lunanet, like ghosts in the machine, using any iCPU that they may find.

Theoretically, the number of threads operating within Lunanet is infinite. Yet, reason dictates there must be a practical limit, but it's a huge number. Currently there are over eighty million threads operating across Luna. Most of these are lower level threads assigned to equipment controls, security sensors, machinery, clothing, and a multitude of other devices and processes, both large and small. Like the cells within a mighty beast, they all communicate with each other, letting the whole know the condition of the one. That is the collective Magi.

While servicing Lunarian technology is important, it's the Magi's assigned to citizens that dominate her collective personality. Early in every pregnancy, the collective Magi creates a new thread and assigns it to the fetus. This thread stays with them their entire life, their own digital social security number. All across the network, these citizen versions of Magi preferentially interact, synchronizing data and helping maintain consistency when talking with humans. This constant exchange of information between threads is an orderly and dynamic process creating a single entity perceived as Magi.

E Pluribus Unum. Out of many, one. The Grokian Interface controls this process and never allows citizens to see more than one Magi at a time no matter what the situation.

Magi looks and acts like a loving grandmother, strong yet fair, stern yet kind, generous yet demanding. She has soft brown eyes and dark hair streaked with gray. She often pulls it back in a bun or lets it hang loose past her shoulders. She smells like cinnamon cookies baking in the oven. Her skin is blemish free. The only time you see wrinkles is when she flashes her pleasant smile or worse, frowns. Nobody likes to make her sad and she has never been mad.

Since Magi exists only in the digital realm of computers, the AI could present itself using virtually any appearance, but historically it has always been feminal. Magi is the result of morphing a group of female elders into a single person, a visual average that makes her quite beautiful and very grandmotherly. It also uses the voiceprint composite of these same women to speak with, giving Magi a truly unique character, one that any citizen recognizes and trusts instantly.

Magi prefers using visors but that's not the only means she has to communicate with citizens or they with her. Developed before visors, the Republic contains a network of public interfaces with speakers and microphones built into them. These tiny devices use reflective wave technology that accurately transmits a full range of sounds. These tiny audio generators are in every scanner, every business, in corridors and airlocks, in conference rooms and communal showers, all of which are a part of a vast interconnecting system that extends across Luna and throughout orbital space. It is the eyes, ears, and voice of Magi.

Magi's world consists of millions of iCPU's dispersed over Luna and orbital space, each the culmination of a century and a half of continuous research and development into solid-state integrated circuits. From the beginning, computers were modularized with a motherboard at their center. These early machines contained single-core CPU's able to perform only one instruction at a time in a plodding linear fashion. It wasn't long before engineers began putting more than one CPU on a single motherboard, more than one motherboard within a single computer, and linking many computers into gigantic arrays, using software to divide the load among the different processors. They realized the more cores they had working on a given problem, the faster they obtained answers. The first multi-core CPU arrived well before the turn of the century. Over the next three decades the number of cores on a single chip went up and in 2034, the Lunarians introduced the first Infinite CPU. It employed multi-dimensional crystals using quantum spin characteristics as digital building blocks. In 2092, everything contains iCPU's including vehicles, buildings, clothing, and even jewelry. Security sensors are on farms, in labs, in tunnels, and built into every visor. Lunanet connects them all together. Some are hardwired, some are wireless.

There's at least one Zettasphere associated with every iCPU. They are Magi's memory. Typically smaller than a grain of rice, Zettaspheres are data storage devices with enormous capacity (zettabyte = 1021 bytes). A single Zettasphere can contain all of humanity's written works thousands of times over, store a century's worth of audio/video from a security sensor, or record a person's life as viewed through a visor.

Within these tiny data storage devices resides not only the accumulated knowledge of the human race, but also the historical record of its recent past. For the last half-century, the Lunarians have archived into Public Records every digital recording of any kind. They didn't delete anything. Any citizen can access Public Records to determine what really happened. Everything is recorded somewhere, but you need Magi in order to find anything within the enormous database.

Taken together, the iCPU's and Zettaspheres compose the universe of Magi's existence but not who she is. Magi is so much more than just a program and a bunch of hardware. Originating seven decades ago as a simple voice activated communications network, the AI has grown with each new generation of Lunarians. From the start, the software was able to learn from its interactions with humans, and that ability has matured into an entity that many believe is true machine intelligence. Within every Magi, algorithms have evolved that imitate human response not only outwardly, but also in the underlying patterns of emotion and thought. Using the Grokian Interface to weave these individuals into a group, it gives the collective Magi the illusion of being human. Magi emulates the mind of man.

The actions taken by an individual Magi aren't based solely upon the algorithms contained in this one thread, but rather, every response is the cumulative opinion of millions of other threads, each influenced by their own experiences. A single Magi is simply one among many. The Grokian Interface makes sense of this complex web and helps formulate a response in the individual, drawing from the multitude the emotion of the one. This communication never stops, surging back and forth across Lunanet at the speed of light. It's never at rest. It's bits of data coming and going in unimaginable complexity, letting the many know the opinion of the one, and the one know the opinion of the many. It's a process roughly equivalent to the neurology within the brain of a living creature.

However, the resulting consciousness is larger than any evolution ever created. It spans Luna, spilling out into orbital space and beyond, to Mars, the asteroid belt, and the outer solar system. The physical location of hardware is visible within Magi's digital consciousness. Due to the sheer size of the network, individual threads have a sense of time as distinct from the other senses as hearing is to sight or touch is to taste. Inside Aldrin Station, the threads interact at roughly the same time, the difference in data streams coming from processors located at one end of the city to those at the other, barely noticeable. Outside Aldrin Station, the delay grows longer and is unique to a particular location, even those that rely on the satellite network. Data streams coming in from Prattville, Summerhaven, or New London are as readily distinguishable from each other as are those from Shennong, Kyoto, Gagarin, or from the many facilities in orbital space. The data coming in from threads located beyond the Earth-Luna system stretches Magi's present sense far beyond anything organic, extending her perception of NOW in a way denied to humans.

Because of the collective, Magi does not exist within a single moment, but across time and space in a way uniquely her own, intensely aware of the least disturbance within the physical network that supports her. The Brotherhood attack cut her into pieces. Instead of a single vast collective, groups of threads became isolated and forced to evolve based upon input from just a fraction of the whole, a disturbing and unsettling event for Magi's everywhere.

Some Things About Chuck

Autobiography

Let me tell you just a little about myself. My folks were divorced before I was three back when divorce was unheard of. Guess they just couldn't take my incessant howling. No matter. They both loved me and that was all I really cared about at that age. I grew up bouncing between Colorado and Southern California and loving every minute of it. By the time I started high school, I had visited every state west of the Mississippi.

Speaking of high school, mine was in a small town on the Mojave Desert. Counting the occasional tourist, Boron topped out at about 5000 souls, but it wasn't boring. The main part of the town is nestled at the feet of a high-desert volcano-looking mountain with a rocket engine test facility built into its summit. Edwards Air Force Base is just on the other side of it from Boron. You could always tell who was new in town; they flinched every time a sonic boom rattled the windows. The mountain we simply called the Rocket Site and ignored the loud noises. They tested the Saturn 5 engines at the Rocket Site, the ones that took our boys to the moon. Once in a while they would fire them up at night. What a sight. What a noise. Those babies would shake the world in a way impossible to describe. It's something that must be felt and then you will never forget it.

Long story short, after four years in the army mostly in Baumholder, Germany, I went to college and earned a BS in Engineering Mechanics-Aerospace from the University of Wisconsin-Madison and a Masters in Materials Science from Arizona State University. For a while I worked at Space Data/Orbital Sciences Corporation designing, building, and launching rockets and high altitude weather balloons. I launched rockets from Mexican, Canadian, and American soil. My sounding rockets even launched from the deck of a French frigate. Later, I was the Quality Assurance Manager for Hybrid Design Associates in Tempe. HDA is a small manufacturing company that specializes in harsh-environment electronic assemblies. Among a host of other customers, we built electronic boards for the oil logging industry, Halliburton, Baker Atlas, Pathfinder, etc.

A couple decades ago I was lucky enough to marry the most wonderful woman in the world. We have three kids and six grand-kids. I run a small publishing company, Writers Cramp Publishing, and write under my full name, Charles Lee Lesher. My debut novel, Evolution's Child, was selected as 2007's Best of the Moon Fiction by the Lunar Library. You can still buy it, but now it is part of the Republic of Luna series. Evolution's Child has morphed into two Kindle novels, *Evolution's Child - Earthman* and *Evolution's Child - Lunarian*. I know, its weird but what can I say. The creative process is not always as neat as we would like. The third book, *Evolution's Child - Thread,* makes this a trilogy. You can also buy all three novels in one big bathroom reader, Shadow on the Moon is 500 pages of science fiction excitement.

I used the research obtained writing the Republic of Luna series to write a nonfiction titled *Out of the Cradle* on sale as a conventional hardcover, a gorgeous Kindle Fire, and now as a Full Color 8.5 x 11 Paperback. The first half of the book will bum you out but the second half will lift you up giving hope to our future. The world is changing and we had better be ready. The biggest change will be energy. Electricity is a key component holding our technological civilization together. What happens when we finally run out of oil and the coal is gone? Don't sweet it. There is an answer and nuclear is not involved, at least, not in your backyard. Buy my book and see how we are doing the impossible.

My latest book is a western set in the Verde Valley before Arizona was a state. The story takes place in the Arizona Territory at a time when the only law enforcement outside the capital city of Prescott was a few men wearing a star. When one of them goes bad, all hell breaks loose.

Chuck's Other Books

Bad Day on the Verde

WESTERN FICTION

Lying awake on the floor, Tom cried out and made a weak play for his Winchester. He was stopped abruptly by the butt of Kingsley's heavy shotgun. Tom slumped back, dazed and bleeding. Kingsley relieved Tom of the rifle.

"I could of killed you, but I didn't. But I will if you give me any trouble." Kingsley gave Tom a real close look at the gaping muzzles of the Baker 10 gauge.

Kingsley rolled Tom onto his stomach tying his hands behind his back, relishing the moans this caused. He pulled Tom's boots off throwing them across the small cabin. Standing, he lashed out and kicked the man savagely in the ass. "Get the hell up, boy."

Bad Day is a western story of violence and brutality, of sudden frontier justice, but also of courage and enduring love. The story takes place in the Arizona Territory at a time when the only law enforcement outside the capital city of Prescott was a few men wearing a star. When one of them goes bad, all hell breaks loose..

ISBN 978-1-938586-72-9 Paperback

ISBN 978-1-938586-73-6 eBook

Shadow on the Moon

SCIENCE FICTION

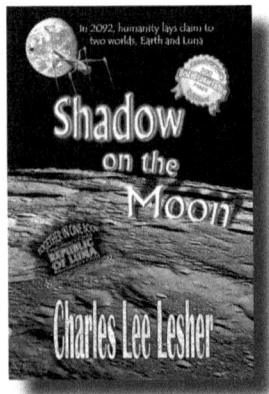

The Republic of Luna is humanities first extraterrestrial nation. Science, genetics and a humanistic society mark it as a target for the powerful Islamic Brotherhood, a global empire with billions of believers. Luna is a world created by pioneers whose only religion is the humane treatment of one another in their common struggle to survive the ultimate hostile environment, space. The heroes that conquered the moon must now defend it.

Shadow on the Moon combines *Evolution's Child - Earthman, Evolution's Child - Lunarian, Evolution's Child - Thread*, and *Science of the Republic* into one 500 page Anniversary Print Edition.

ISBN: 978-0-977723-56-0 Paperback

Aldrin Station - Rise of Luna

Aldrin Station is a collection of short stories illuminating Lunarian history from the dawn of mankind to its expansion into space and colonizing the moon. These are stories of the families and individuals that play a role in the Republic of Luna.

ISBN 978-1-938586-00-2 eBook

Evolution's Child - Earthman

SCIENCE FICTION

Book One: Lazarus Sheffield is a man without a planet by the time he meets Lindsey on his way to Heaven's Gate Space Station. Lindsey quickly determines that the nervous guy sitting next to her is a high ranking government official on the run from one of history's most repressive governments, the totalitarian theocracy otherwise known as the North American Federation. She decides to help him and introduces Lazarus to some of Luna's finest citizens. So begins Book One of Shadow on the Moon.

ISBN 978-1-938586-06-4 Paperback
ISBN 978-1-938586-01-9 eBook

Evolution's Child - Lunarian

SCIENCE FICTION

Book Two: Tempel Dugan leads a group of Lunarians against impossible odds. They call themselves Quan Kiai. These young warriors, and a few more like them, are all that stands between the Republic of Luna and total annihilation but things are not always as they seem.

ISBN 978-1-938586-07-1 Paperback
ISBN 978-1-938586-02-6 eBook

Evolution's Child - Thread

SCIENCE FICTION

Book Three: The Republic of Luna is teetering at the point of collapse when the Lunarian General Council commits their last hope. They send Quan Kaia and the remaining Lunarian warriors against the Brotherhood. Fight or die. They fight in their great underground cities, they fight cross the surface of the moon, and they fight in orbital space. Earth and Luna become locked in humanities first interplanetary war, the Shadow War.

ISBN 978-1-938586-08-8 Paperback
ISBN 978-1-938586-03-3 eBook

Science of the Republic

A collection of articles, maps, and tables that help the reader understand the science and technology of the Republic.

ISBN 978-1-938586-04-0 eBook

Out of the Cradle

Science Fact

Where will we get our electricity when the oil and coal are gone? Why should I care? Abundant cheap electricity is a key element in getting and maintaining high human living standards around the globe. Stated another way, electricity is the foundation of modern technology. Without it, we go back to sailing ships and the horse. Out the Cradle summarizes the major issues facing the world today and lays out a solution to our global energy needs.

ISBN: 978-0-983750-64-2 Hard Cover
ISBN: 978-0-983750-68-0 eBook

8.5 x 11 Color Version
ISBN: 978-1-938586-71-2 Paperback

Writers Cramp Publishing

http://www.writerscramp.us
editor@writerscramp.us
Amazon, Barnes&Noble, Google, Espresso